The

He'll need ___ ___ ___use!

Two billion___ ___ ___ ___ they want get more than they bargained for when their exes return—each with a baby in tow!

Will they stop playing the field and play happy families?

Find out in these two intense and passionate stories from two *USA TODAY* bestselling authors, Jennie Lucas and Kate Hewitt.

JENNIE LUCAS grew up dreaming about faraway lands. At fifteen, hungry for experience beyond the borders of her small Idaho city, she went to a Connecticut boarding school on scholarship. She took her first solo trip to Europe at sixteen, then put off college and traveled around the U.S., supporting herself with jobs as diverse as gas-station cashier and newspaper advertising assistant. At twenty-two, she met the man who would be her husband. After their marriage she graduated from Kent State University with a degree in English. Seven years after she started writing she got the magical call from London that turned her into a published author. Since then, life has been hectic, with a new writing career, a sexy husband and two small children, but she's having a wonderful (albeit sleepless) time. She loves immersing herself in dramatic, glamorous, passionate stories. Maybe she can't physically travel to Morocco or Spain right now, but for a few hours a day, while her children are sleeping, she can be there in her books. Jennie loves to hear from her readers. You can visit her website at www.jennielucas.com, or drop her a note at jennie@jennielucas.com.

KATE HEWITT discovered her first Harlequin® romance on a trip to England when she was thirteen, and she's continued to read them ever since. She wrote her first story at the age of five, simply because her older brother had written one and she thought she could do it, too. That story was one sentence long—fortunately, they've become a bit more detailed as she's grown older. She has written plays, short stories and magazine serials for many years, but writing romance remains her first love. Besides writing, she enjoys reading, traveling and learning to knit. After marrying the man of her dreams—her older brother's childhood friend—she lived in England for six years. She now resides in Connecticut with her husband, her three young children, and the possibility of one day getting a dog. Kate loves to hear from readers. You can contact her through her website, www.kate-hewitt.com.

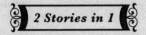

2 Stories in 1

Jennie Lucas
Kate Hewitt

THE SECRET BABY SCANDAL

Harlequin®

TORONTO NEW YORK LONDON
AMSTERDAM PARIS SYDNEY HAMBURG
STOCKHOLM ATHENS TOKYO MILAN MADRID
PRAGUE WARSAW BUDAPEST AUCKLAND

Recycling programs
for this product may
not exist in your area.

ISBN-13: 978-0-373-13015-3

THE SECRET BABY SCANDAL

First North American Publication 2011

The publisher acknowledges the copyright holders
of the individual works as follows:

THE COUNT'S SECRET CHILD
Copyright © 2011 by Jennie Lucas

THE SANDOVAL BABY
Copyright © 2011 by Kate Hewitt

CONTENTS

THE COUNT'S SECRET CHILD

Jennie Lucas

CHAPTER ONE

HOLDING her sleeping baby against her chest, Carrie Powell looked up at the French castle in the moonlit night. She shivered as a warm breeze blew tendrils of hair across her hot skin.

After a year of cold silence, Théo St. Raphaël, Comte de Castelnau, had finally sent for her. He finally wished to meet their three-month-old son.

Carrie's shivering intensified as she stared up at the castle where Théo had first seduced her, before he'd abandoned her in Seattle two weeks later, leaving her pregnant and alone.

Once, she'd loved him more than life. She'd thought he was her knight in shining armor, this titled tycoon who'd made his own fortune. She'd loved him with blind, girlish devotion—her only lover, the only man she could even imagine loving.

Carrie took a shaking breath. She'd been such a fool.

Growing up, her older brothers had rolled their eyes at the way she saw the best in people. Even her parents had teased her—dreamy, cheerful Carrie with her head in the clouds, who defended people who cut in line at the supermarket or were rude for no reason at all. But those people were doing the best they could, Carrie thought. The grumpy woman who cut in line at the grocery store might have some private tragedy or worry she could hardly bear. Carrie tried to like everyone. She'd maybe disliked one or two truly unpleasant people in her life, but she'd certainly never *hated* anyone.

Until now.

"Come, *mademoiselle*," the bodyguard said, holding out the baby seat he'd taken from the luxury sedan as the driver retrieved her luggage from the trunk. "We are late."

Grabbing the handle of the baby carrier, she glared at him, then sighed. He'd practically kidnapped her from her parents' house, but the man was just doing his job. The one she really blamed was his boss.

Setting the baby carrier down on the cool grass, she gently tucked her sleeping baby inside the padded frame and wrapped a warm blanket around him. She certainly hadn't planned on Henry wearing footsie pajamas when he was introduced to his father for the first time, but the baby was exhausted and had only slept an hour on the private jet. An hour more than Carrie had.

Every muscle in her body felt tight as she rose back to her feet, lifting the handle of the baby carrier to gently sway her baby back and forth.

After deserting her when she needed him the most, yesterday Théo had sent his bodyguard to collect her without even the courtesy of a phone call. But what should she expect of a man so selfish, so ruthless, so cold?

Thank heaven she'd stopped loving Théo long ago. There was only one thing left between them now. One thing that mattered. Emotion choked Carrie's throat as she looked down at the downy head of her tiny sleeping baby nestled against his soft blue blanket.

Even though she hated Théo with all her heart, she would not deny him the chance to meet his son.

The bodyguard held the door open, waiting for her. *"Mademoiselle, s'il vous plaît."*

Carrie stared past him into the dark entrance of the castle, suddenly nervous. She glanced at the bodyguard. "You will stay with us?"

The man shook his head. "He wants to see you alone."

Alone. Carrie bit her lip. "But you'll be back in the morning to collect me?" she persisted. "Or sooner? Later tonight?"

The man's face was blank. "That is as Monsieur le Comte wishes."

Monsieur le Comte? Had she just gone back in time to some feudal age where everyone trembled and obeyed Théo as master? Carrie took a deep breath, clenching her hands into fists. Well, not her. There'd be no more trembling and no more obeying. She would go into Gavaudan Castle and be coldly polite. She'd show Théo the beautiful child he'd unthinkingly rejected, and by this time tomorrow he'd be bored with them both. She and Henry would be on their way back to Seattle, secure in the knowledge that Théo would never trouble them again.

Lifting her chin, Carrie gripped the handle of the baby carrier and slowly walked inside the darkened foyer. Her feet felt as heavy as bricks. Once inside, she heard the crystal chandelier chiming discordantly above them and terror seized her heart.

Her hands shook so violently she set the baby carrier down on the marble floor as she turned back with desperation. "But, really, I don't mind if you stay—"

"Bon courage, mademoiselle," the bodyguard said.

The driver set her luggage inside the foyer and the men closed the door behind her with a sonorous bang.

Carrie was alone inside the castle. With her baby. And with Théo. Her hands shook as she looked around, trying to calm her fiercely beating heart.

The shadows of the silent castle were all around her. As she looked at all the dark hallways leading off the foyer, memories went through her like waves. She heard the echoes of their playful lovers' laughter, like ghosts of their former happiness.

Down that hall, she remembered, Théo had fed her strawberries and champagne in the glorious warmth and flowers of the summer garden. Through that door, in the two-story library, he'd read her poems in French. She'd felt the dark heat of Théo's eyes, heard the beauty of the language as it shaped his beautiful, sensual lips. She hadn't understood his words, but she'd known their meaning: desire.

Carrie's eyes fell on the sweeping staircase. He'd carried her up those stairs as if she weighed nothing at all. He'd laid her upon his enormous bed and he'd seduced her, taking her virginity, kissing and suckling and soaring her to the heights of ecstasy. She wrapped her arms around her jean jacket. She could still feel his arms, feel his lips, feel his hard muscular body against hers as he'd pressed her back on the bed and caressed her naked skin as she trembled and shook and cried out beneath him....

She heard a noise behind her, and whirled around with a low gasp.

Théo St. Raphaël, Comte de Castelnau and lord of Gavaudan Castle, stood in the open doorway, his powerful body a dark shadow.

"Théo." She whispered his name with the French pronunciation—hard *T*, silent *H*.

He was breathtaking, almost terrifying in his masculine beauty. He was so dark. Black hair, black trousers, black shirt open at the neck. Dark stubble covered the hard line of his jaw. But it was the expression in his piercing eyes that was darkest of all.

Across the shadowy foyer, his black eyes glittered at her. *"Enfin."*

His low, deep voice went through her like a hot knife through her heart. Carrie couldn't move. Couldn't even breathe as he moved toward her, stalking her, never taking his eyes from hers.

"I have waited." Stopping in front of her, he looked down at her. "For too long," he murmured, "I have wanted you."

She could hardly believe she was standing in front of him now, close enough to feel the warmth of his body. She had to tilt her head way back to look up into his hard, handsome face. Théo. A lump rose in her throat. Théo, in the flesh. The man she'd once loved, the man who'd left her, the man who'd dropped her so completely he'd never even given her the chance to tell him she was pregnant.

For almost a year Carrie had dreamed of what she would say to him if she ever saw him again. She had a little speech prepared, practiced many times during long, lonely nights, that she planned to deliver in the same cold, dispassionate tone that he'd used when he'd left her that morning in the hotel room.

But in the shock of the moment her entire speech fled from her mind. She felt overwhelmed by the intensity of his closeness. Her body trembled from her hair to her earlobes to her toes as she looked into his darkly handsome face.

He reached out a hand and stroked along the top edge of her shoulder, over her jean jacket, up her neck to her cheek. Cupping her face, he tilted up her chin, and she couldn't fight. Couldn't even protest. She just trembled.

"Now, at last," he whispered, lowering his mouth to hers, "you will be mine."

And, ruthlessly, he kissed her.

His lips were hot and hard against hers, bruising her mouth, sending sparks of electric current sizzling down the length of her body. As one of his hands roughly cupped her chin, his other arm wrapped around her body, holding her tight, pressing her breasts against his muscular chest. She felt trapped, overpowered by the strength of his body, by the force of his overwhelming hunger. And out of nowhere she suddenly realized that, against her will, she was kissing him back.

His lips gentled against hers, caressing and luring where a moment before they had demanded and roughly taken. She felt his tongue flick against hers, luring her into a deeper sensuality as his hand stroked lightly against the skin of her cheek. She felt feminine, vulnerable beneath his masculine power.

His hand tilted back her head, exposing her throat. His fingers moved through her hair as he kissed down her neck. A gasp of surrender escaped her as his lips moved down her skin. His caress was smooth as silk, his jawline and upper lip rough as sandpaper, and as he nipped at the sensitive corner between her neck and shoulder all her nerve endings sizzled. Her breathing was hoarse and she sagged in his arms. Her eyes were closed, her body shivering with need from a year of repressed, agonized desire.

"I missed you, *ma petite*," Théo whispered, his lips brushing her ear. "And I see you missed me."

She'd missed him?

Carrie's eyes flew open at his smug male satisfaction. She remembered months of ignored messages, the nights she'd spent sobbing for him with a broken heart after he'd deserted her without explanation. Pride stiffened her body. With a gasp, she ripped away from him, drawing back her hand in fury.

But before she could give him the slap he deserved he caught her wrist. Amusement twisted his sensual lips. "So you did not miss me quite as much as I missed you, *hein*?"

Glaring at him, she yanked her hand from his grasp, angry at the way he'd kissed her—and the way she'd allowed him to do it! He clearly believed she was still the naïve girl she'd been last year—still ripe for the taking, still putty in his hands! He obviously assumed she'd spent the past year dreaming of him. And she *hadn't* dreamed of him. Not for weeks now!

She lifted her chin furiously. "You think you can just kiss me and I'll swoon into your arms?"

He lifted a dark eyebrow. "No?"

Carrie sucked in her breath at the arrogant expression on his wickedly handsome face. "You have no right to kiss me. No right to even touch me!"

"Perhaps I have no right." Looking at her, he gave a low laugh. "But you are here."

"You left me no choice—your bodyguard gave me no notice!"

"He asked you to come to Gavaudan, and you agreed." Reaching out, Théo took her hand. She tried to resist, but he was too strong. She felt the sizzling heat of his palm against hers and a sizzle spread down her skin. "And what am I to make of that, *chérie*, except that you have wanted me just as I have wanted you?"

"*Wanted* me?" Her voice shook with incredulous anger. "You left without a word and never returned any of my messages—for a year!"

He reached out a hand to stroke her cheek. "I never stopped wanting you, Carrie," he said in a low voice. "I left because you broke the rules. But I think we both understand each other now. This time there will be no more talk of love, yes?"

A bitter laugh escaped her. "Believe me. There is absolutely *no way* I'd ever love you again."

"Good." He smiled. "In that case, there is no reason for us to be apart. No reason for us to continue to suffer from unrequited desire." His hands slowly moved down her shoulders, stroking her arms, over her white denim jacket. Stroking back her long brown hair, he lowered his head toward hers, whispering huskily, "I have never forgotten how it felt to have you in my bed…"

He was going to kiss her. Why couldn't she push away from him? Why couldn't her body even make a single move to safety?

A sudden plaintive wail came from the shadows near the doorway, and Théo straightened with a frown. "What was that?"

Carrie exhaled, grateful beyond measure that her baby had saved her from herself. "The only reason I'm here."

The furrows in his forehead deepened. "What do you mean?"

She turned away. "I'll get him."

Going to the doorway, she lifted her son out of the baby carrier. Henry's wail ended with a snuffle as soon as he was snug in her arms. But when she returned to Théo he didn't look pleased. He looked shocked and bewildered. "Why did you bring a baby here?"

She frowned in her turn. "Did you think I would refuse to bring him?" She stroked the back of the tiny warm baby cuddled up against her chest. "This is Henry, Théo. Your son."

His mouth fell open. His dark eyes, usually so arrogant and certain, were wide with shock as he staggered back from her.

"My son?" he gasped. *"My son!"*

She heard the harsh rattle of his breath, saw the way his hands clenched into fists. Then, with visible self-control, he exhaled, relaxing his hands.

"Are you trying to claim," he ground out, "that we have a child together?"

Confused and heartsick, she looked up at him. "But you know that," she whispered. "Someone already told you about Henry. Why else would you have sent for me?"

Their eyes locked. Above them in the shadowy foyer she heard the discordant chime of the chandelier, blown by an unseen wind.

"That baby cannot be mine," Théo said through clenched teeth. "It is impossible."

"Yes, I thought so," she said helplessly. "But contraception is not one hundred percent effective—"

He paced in front of her like a lion in a cage. "You are lying to me. Why?" He whirled on her, baring his teeth. "Is this some kind of revenge?"

Carrie gasped aloud. "Revenge? How?"

"An attempt to trick me." He clawed a hand back through his dark hair. "To trap me into marriage!"

"Marriage—with *you*?" She gave an incredulous laugh. "No way!"

"So you say. But women always want to marry me," he said coldly. "I thought you were different. I'm disappointed."

He stared at her as if she were dirt—and didn't even *look* at the baby who'd traveled five thousand miles to meet him. With a trembling breath, she looked up at him.

"Let me make myself clear in a way that even your huge ego won't misunderstand." Her eyes narrowed. "I don't want to marry you. I *hate* you."

Théo stared at her.

"Hate," she emphasized.

Setting his jaw, he shook his head in disbelief. "Then why would you come here?"

She lifted her chin. "Because I thought even a bastard like you deserved to meet his child. When you sent your bodyguard to collect me like that I assumed you'd heard about our baby. What else would you want from me?"

He looked down at her, his black eyes like fire. Then, with a low growl, he grabbed her free arm. Pulling her down the hallway, he led her out through the back door.

Outside in the moonlight she saw the shadows of trees stretching up into the violet sky. In the garden, a table for two was lit by white candles. Dozens of roses surrounded the table.

"For this," he said harshly.

Shocked, Carrie took in the romantic scene, her eyes wide. She looked back at him. "You intended to seduce me?" she breathed.

Théo's eyes were pools of molten heat. "Yes."

A cold chill of fury went down her spine. She swept her arm toward the table. "You thought this was all it would take? That I would fall instantly into your bed?"

He came closer to her, his black eyes searing hers. "Yes."

Her skin felt warm all over, being this near to him. She shivered as memories raced through her.

He'd swept her off her feet in a whirlwind affair. On their third date, a week after they'd met, he'd whisked her to his *château* via private jet and seduced her. But after the weekend was over he'd sent her back to Seattle, alone. Two weeks later he'd come back to the Emerald City for business and invited her to his downtown hotel.

She'd gone so eagerly. She almost wept to remember it now. She'd rushed to his penthouse suite like a girl whose sailor had just come into port.

He hadn't sent for her now in order to finally meet Henry. All Théo wanted was a booty call—and he'd had her delivered to his house like a pizza. Racked with pain, she closed her eyes.

She felt his hand on her shoulder. Spreading his fingers wide, he stroked the bare skin of her collarbone and neck.

Carrie's eyes flew open. She jerked away so fast that Henry gave a startled cry.

"I brought my baby across the world for you, and all you've done is insult me—and reject him." She blinked back tears. She would not cry in front of him, she *would not*. "Thank you, Théo, for setting me free. As of this moment, I no longer consider you Henry's father."

His eyebrows lowered into a furious scowl. "Carrie—"

"Once I would have given you everything," she whispered. She lifted her chin and her eyes glittered in the moonlight. "Now...you will have nothing."

CHAPTER TWO

THÉO St. Raphaël had learned long ago how destructive the idea of love could be.

Love was a pretty fantasy, in his opinion. And yet it ruined real lives—especially when children were involved. A man and woman would imagine themselves *in love*, and in the throes of passion decide to have a child; but then just as quickly, after the baby was born, they'd realize they weren't in love after all, and go elsewhere looking for that passionate, all-consuming fantasy. Leaving a young child without a real home, living with stepparents and half-siblings like a third wheel or a poor relation, tolerated at best.

When the love that created a child died, that child would never feel really home—anywhere in the world.

Not that Théo knew the feeling, of course. It was true his aristocratic French father and young American mother had divorced when he was eight, but he remembered that as a blessing. They'd fought constantly—his father cruel and sarcastic, his mother weeping helplessly—when they'd once been desperately in love.

As a child, he'd felt relieved when they'd finally split—his father to Paris, his mother to Chicago—and started shuttling their only son between them. His mother had quickly married again and soon had new children, another family. She was now on her fourth husband, while Théo's father had simply given up the idea of marriage and instead kept mistresses half his age.

Love was a narcotic, Théo thought, that barely lasted longer than a cigarette. Who would be foolish enough to base marriage on such a feeling? A marriage, a home, should be run like a business. It deserved to be treated with the same care.

He'd always assumed that sometime around the age of forty—four years from now—he would select a woman to be his wife based upon her intelligence, beauty and her capacity for child-rearing, and initiate a merger. They both would enjoy the strengths of a solid home, assets such as companionship, partnership and sex. There would be no talk of *love*, an emotion no one could quantify and which would inevitably evaporate like smoke.

Théo hadn't wanted children until he could give them a true home—a rock-solid foundation that would last for life. He'd always known how his life would be.

He'd never expected this.

"This is Henry, Théo. Your son."

Carrie was lying, of course. She had to be lying. It was impossible. He'd always used a condom when they'd made love.

And yet…

He looked at her in the moonlit garden. Her big hazel eyes were dark in the shadows, almost haunted in the pale, beautiful face beneath the waves of her glossy chestnut hair. In her white jacket, tank top and floaty skirt, he saw that her slim figure had rounded into womanly curves that made it difficult for him to look away from her body. So he forced himself to look back into her guarded, resentful eyes.

The girl he'd known in Seattle had been a sweet, idealistic, fierce dreamer—an impractical young woman who worked as a waitress by day, scribbled poetry by night, lived with her parents and had a head full of fairytales. It had taken him a full week to seduce her—which was unusual for his affairs. And when he'd finally taken her in his bed upstairs he'd discovered the reason for her shyness: he'd been her first lover.

Théo still shuddered with the intense heat of the memory. Their time together had been far too short. Just a weekend here, then a night in Seattle weeks later, when he'd concluded the acquisition of a Japanese shipping company. Their brief affair had been the most amazing sexual experience of his life, and God knew he had a lot to compare it with. He'd never wanted it to end.

Then she'd ruined everything.

Carrie had been lying in his arms in bed, after a full night making love in his hotel suite. She'd suddenly looked up at him in the slanted gray light of a misty Seattle morning and out of nowhere she'd whispered, "I love you, Théo."

Within seconds he'd been out of the bed and in the shower. He'd gotten dressed without answering any of her bewildered questions. Ten minutes later he'd checked out of his hotel room and was en route to the airport.

He'd known he would never see Carrie again. He'd told himself he didn't care. No matter how mind-blowing the sex had been, he'd soon forget her—like all the rest.

Except he hadn't. Not even close.

For the past year, no matter how spectacular his conquests—either in business or with women—he'd been eternally unsatisfied. Worst of all, it had started to affect his work. Recently he'd bought a steel business in Rio de Janeiro at a loss, taking it from his rival by overbidding a huge amount. He'd thought the empty gnawing in his gut would be filled by stealing the family business from his longtime rival Gabriel Santos.

Instead, all he'd gained was an aging Brazilian steel

company he didn't really want, and the knowledge that he'd wasted a great deal of money to get it. Even splitting up the most profitable divisions of Açoazul S.A. wouldn't compensate him for the price he'd paid. And he'd lost one of his finest vineyards in Champagne in the deal.

He'd won, only to discover that he'd lost.

Finally, Théo had surrendered to his body's demands. He'd sent for Carrie to propose a no-strings affair. He'd rationalized that she'd learned her lesson and would know never to mention the word *love* to him again.

He'd never expected a child.

And right now Théo saw the child being walked straight out the door in his mother's arms.

"Wait," he said harshly.

Carrie paused at the door, not looking back at him.

"If he is really my son," he ground out, "why didn't you tell me? How could you have kept him secret for a year?"

"Secret!" she gasped, whirling around in fury. "I left messages for months, *begging* you to call me!"

He set his jaw. "I ignored your messages because I thought you would repeat words I have no interest in hearing. I didn't want you to embarrass yourself. Or me."

Carrie's cheeks went red. "I *am* embarrassed," she whispered. Blinking fast, she looked away. "I'm ashamed every time I remember how much I loved you."

Looking at her beautiful face, at the tight posture of her body as she held the baby against her chest, Théo felt a strange emotion—one he barely recognized.

Guilt.

Furious, he glared at her. "We had a deal, Carrie. From the day we met you knew I only wanted a physical affair, nothing more. You are the one who betrayed that. You are the one who crossed the line."

She opened her mouth, then closed it again. She took a

deep breath. "You're right," she said in a low voice. "We did have a deal. But I was too much of an innocent to know how making love to you would bind my heart. And I didn't realize you'd be able to toss me aside so easily the moment I admitted my feelings." Her voice trembled and she looked away. "The next man I love will be different," she whispered. "He will be honest and strong. He will love me back."

The next man I love. A low sense of unease went through Théo's soul like a roll of distant thunder. *The next man I love.* The thought of Carrie taking a lover disquieted him. More than disquieted. Enraged. He tried to push away the feeling. Jealousy was just another form of weakness—of attachment.

He set his jaw, focusing on the facts. "Let me see the baby."

With visible reluctance, Carrie turned her shoulder so he could see the baby in the moonlight. He frowned down at the child she'd called his son. It was possible, he admitted to himself grudgingly. The child had dark hair. But all babies looked more or less the same, didn't they, with plump cheeks and big eyes?

"Your bodyguard didn't even mention him?" she asked quietly.

He looked up at Carrie abruptly. "He did call about a complication. But I told him I didn't give a damn. I just wanted you here." He paused. "I just wanted *you…*"

Carrie's wide-set hazel eyes looked up at him, limpid and clear as a mountain lake beneath the moonlight of the garden. Théo felt a current of electricity sizzle down his body. He still wanted her. More than ever. Licking his lips, he took a single step toward her.

She held out her hand. "No," she whispered. She stepped back from him, her lips twisting bitterly as she glanced back at the table of candles and roses. "There will be no seduction. I'll never be yours again. I'm here only for Henry."

With a deep breath, he looked down at the child in her arms. "You named him Henry? After your father?"

She nodded. "Henry Powell."

Théo blinked. Then he sucked in his breath as he looked at her, his eyes wide with shock. "You claim he is mine, but you did not give him my name?"

Her eyes narrowed. "You didn't deserve it."

The depth of the insult was a slap across the jaw. If there was any chance the baby *was* his son...

"I want to get a paternity test," he said harshly. "Until I have proof either way, both you and the child will stay."

She went pale. She swallowed.

"No," she whispered. "I don't want to stay here. I won't."

He exhaled. "So you admit you were lying? The baby will fail the test."

She stiffened, her eyes looking large and luminous in the moonlight. "He won't fail. He's your son. But I wish to God he weren't. All I want now is for us both to be free of you forever." She turned her face, looking wistfully out into the night. "And we were so close..."

Free of him?

Théo stared at her in shock. *Free of him.* What a strange idea. Women always tried to stay in his life as long as possible. They wept when he left. And yet Carrie Powell was acting as if she truly didn't want him in her life—or her child's.

It wasn't a pretense or a game. He saw that in her eyes. She was truly praying that he would let her go.

"If I'm really his father," he said evenly, "I have no choice but to take responsibility."

"You haven't taken responsibility for a year, and we've all been very happy without you," she said coolly.

"I don't think you understand," he bit out. "I would take care of the child. Financially."

"I'm not interested in your money. I just want to go home."

"If Henry is my son, your home is here."

With an intake of breath, she looked around the fragrant green garden and shook her head. "There's no love here."

For a long moment their eyes locked. The two of them seemed suspended in time. Above them, unseen night birds sang mournfully from the black trees against the violet horizon, and his heart slowed in his chest.

Then his lip curled. "You would decide a baby's fate on something that does not last? You would base your life on a fantasy like *love*?"

"It's not a fantasy!" she cried. "It's real. Love is the only thing that makes a home!"

Scornfully, he shook his head, exhaling with a flare of his nostrils. "I'm not letting you leave until I have proof whether or not he is my son."

Her eyes went wide, as if he'd just suggested she swim naked in a crocodile-infested moat. "But a paternity test could take days! Weeks!"

Théo suspected that for the right price he could have an answer far sooner than that, but he didn't share that information with her. "However long it takes, you will stay."

Trembling, she lifted her chin. "You can't keep me here."

"No?"

"This isn't the Dark Ages. I'm not some serf on your estate, Monsieur le Comte. You can't hold me against my will, I'm not your slave!"

Théo's lips curved upward. "Slave? No." He came toward her. He saw the effort it took for her to stand her ground as he bent and whispered, "But I could make you my prisoner."

He felt her tremble as his lips brushed against the flesh of her ear. Satisfied, he drew away.

She shrank back, even as she tried to toss her head. "I'm not afraid of you."

"You should be." He walked around her, slowly looking her up and down. "Do you understand what I do for a living? How I've made my fortune?"

"You buy struggling companies and break them up for parts. For profit."

"*Oui*. I buy things. I buy people." He paused. "That family you love so much in Seattle. What do you think I could do to them if I chose?"

She sucked in her breath, searching his gaze. "Nothing!"

He lifted a tranquil dark eyebrow. "Nothing?"

"It's an empty threat! You couldn't touch them!"

He looked down at her in amusement. "You really *are* an innocent." He tilted his head thoughtfully. "Do you have any idea of the influence I could wield against…*peut-être*…the bank that holds your parents' loans? Or the companies that employ your brothers?"

Carrie closed her eyes, taking a deep breath near her baby's soft dark hair. When she opened her eyes, they were full of grief. "To think I once loved you. I was a fool to ever think you were a knight in shining armor, or even a decent man."

The same strange pang went through his chest. He pushed the feeling away, setting his jaw. "Decide."

"I won't let you blackmail me. I'm not afraid of you." She lifted her chin. "I'm leaving. Go ahead. Do your worst."

"So brave," he murmured, "and so reckless. It would be better for you to give in to my wishes. Keep your family safe. Does one of your brothers need a job, perhaps? A loan? A gift? I could be a valuable friend."

"You're no one's friend."

"And all I want in return," he said silkily, "is for you to stay here at the *château* until we get the results of a paternity test. Surely that is not so unreasonable?"

He felt her hesitate, felt her caught between her hatred for him and her love for her family. Slowly she lifted her eyes to his. They were hazel-green, like a cool, shadowy forest.

"Why are you doing this?" she said in a low voice. "We both know you have no interest in being a real father to Henry. You've barely looked at him—"

He held out his arms. "Give him to me."

Instinctively she tightened her hold on the baby. Then she gave a sigh and, as he'd known she would, came toward him, her expression resigned. She hesitated, then gently placed the baby in his arms, against his chest.

"Lean back a bit," she said anxiously. "Be sure to support his head—yes. Like that. Good." She paused. "Have you ever held a baby before?"

"No."

"So you're a natural," she said softly. She looked from Théo to the baby in his arms, and a smile traced her pink lips.

His heart did a strange twist in his chest. She hated him, perhaps—but he saw how much she loved this baby.

Théo looked down at Henry and gently stroked his dark, downy head. The baby frowned up at him, bemused. Théo almost laughed. The expression made the baby look almost exactly like Théo's father, when he'd lost his glasses. The baby blinked, then returned his smile. And Théo suddenly lost his breath.

Could this child really be his son? Slowly he looked up at Carrie, his jaw set. "You will allow me to take a paternity test." It was a statement, not a question.

She sighed. "I'm telling you the truth. You're the only man who could be his father."

"How can you be so sure?" he demanded.

Her dark eyelashes fluttered against her pale cheeks as she looked down at the ground. She said, in a voice almost too quiet to hear, "Because you're the only man I've ever... been with."

He looked at her in shock. The only man? *Ever?*

Blinking, she lifted her gaze. "But someday I will find another," she whispered. "I'll find a man who will never abandon me or break my heart."

Théo's body stiffened. There it was again, her mention of a dream man, a perfect masculine paragon that Théo was already beginning to despise.

"Don't bother thinking of him," he said sharply. "If you're telling me the truth, and Henry is my son, you will soon be my wife."

Carrie stared at him, her eyes wide. For several seconds she struggled to speak. Then she choked out, "No!"

"You would put your hatred of me, and your selfish longings for romance, over the best interests of our son?"

Her lips turned down at the edges, and if possible she looked still more unhappy. "I'm not marrying you. Not when I know you will lose interest in being a father within a week—"

"You don't know that," he interrupted fiercely.

"Yes, I do. I know exactly the kind of man you are," she said steadily. "A playboy who doesn't want to ever be tied down, who lives entirely for his own selfish needs, who will never be faithful to any woman for longer than a week."

"Don't you dare presume to—"

"Marriage is a lifelong commitment—until death. It can only be based on love." Her voice hardened. "And I despise you."

Her words burned inside him, echoing and reverberating inside his soul. Once Carrie had looked at him with eyes full of adoration. Now she seemed to hate the sight of him.

Théo looked down at the small baby cuddling against his

chest. The thought of some other, no doubt more deserving man raising his baby son felt like a knife in his throat.

"Henry will live with me in Seattle," she said in a calmer tone. "He'll be surrounded by people who love him. If you truly care about him, you will let him have a home." She hesitated. "I'll let you visit him whenever you wish."

"Merci beaucoup," he ground out.

Reaching over to the baby still in Théo's arms, Carrie stroked her son's back through his soft fleece pajamas. Lifting her gaze, she met Théo's eyes. "You held me to the promise that our affair would be no more than a no-strings affair. If I had held you to the same standard I never would have given you this chance."

He set his jaw. "What? The chance to know of his existence before you try to take him from me forever?"

"In Seattle I can give Henry a family who loves him. I can give him a real home."

"In your parents' rickety little house? While you support him as a waitress?"

Her cheeks went pink. "My family might not be rich but at least we don't try to buy or sell people." She shook her head fiercely. "I know what matters in life in a way you never will. And I'm telling you I'll die before I'll become your wife—paternity test or no."

Théo saw the determined set of her expression and knew that his earlier threat to keep her prisoner was indeed empty. He might be ruthless, but he was no monster. Even if Henry proved to be his son, he couldn't force Carrie to marry him against her will. He couldn't hold her in the dungeon until she came to her senses, no matter what his Provençal ancestors might have done.

He would have to use less brutal means of persuasion.

"You must stay," he said abruptly. "Surely you can see that."

She bit her lip. "What's the longest you think the test could take?"

"A month?" he hedged.

"A month? Forget it! There are labs in the States. We'll go back to Seattle and—"

"Or less. Certainly less. No more than a week, perhaps."

She pressed her lips together, looking from Théo to the baby, who was starting to whine. Was the child hungry? he wondered. Thirsty? Tired? Who knew?

With a sigh, Carrie took the baby from his arms. "And if I do stay," she said hesitantly, sounding as if the words were being ripped out of her by force, "you will leave my family in peace?"

He nodded. "You have my word." He looked at her. "So you agree?"

She set her jaw, considering, then tossed her head. "I would spend a week with the devil himself to get you out of our lives!"

A wave of triumph washed over him. *"Parfait."*

He extended his hand to shake on the deal. When she reluctantly placed her smaller hand in his, he pulled her close. He kissed both her cheeks. He breathed in the sweet fragrance of her soft, warm skin, felt the tremble of her fingers intertwined with his.

And he wanted her. More than he'd ever wanted any woman.

Perhaps he couldn't be her knight in shining armor. But if Henry *was* his child Théo would show Carrie how wrongly she'd judged his character. He would be the most devoted father on earth. And he would marry his baby's mother—by any means necessary.

He placed his hand on the small of her back to lead her back inside. Her cheeks were pink as she jerked away, glaring at him accusingly.

"I was just going to take you to your room," he said innocently.

"I know my way upstairs," she snapped.

He stared after her as she walked ahead with the baby. He knew why she'd reacted so violently to his touch. He'd known it from the moment he kissed her.

Hatred or no hatred, she wanted him as much as he wanted her. He could barely wait to have her in his bed again, to caress her body until her skin was pink as her cheeks, to feel her soft, sweet naked body writhe beneath him as she moaned his name.

She pushed open the door to go back inside, and as he followed her he watched the unconsciously sensual sway of her hips.

He had one week to show Carrie how good a loveless marriage could be.

And if he got his wish the first place he'd show her was bed.

CHAPTER THREE

THE next morning, Carrie pushed open the blue shutters of her bedroom.

Soft sunlight glowed golden across the patchwork of fields of sunflowers and lavender and vines stretching back to the distant cragged mountains. She took a deep breath of fresh cool air, closing her eyes as she felt the sun against her face.

She'd made it through the night. She'd started to fear morning would never come. She'd woken constantly, restless with fear that Théo might come to seduce her. When she'd finally slept, he'd invaded her dreams. *I love you, Carrie,* he'd whispered huskily against her skin. His naked body had been hard and hot against her own. *I've always loved you.*

She'd woken up with a start in the middle of the night to find herself alone in the large bed, her body flushed with heat, her sheets tangled at her feet and her heart pounding with desire. Sitting up, she'd slowly looked around the room, with its wrought-iron bed and antique lady's desk with a vase of roses he'd had brought from the garden. Carrie had wrapped her arms around herself as she'd listened to her baby's deep, even breathing in the nearby crib. The dream had felt so real. If Théo could only love her…

She'd choked out a bitter laugh. Love her? The idea that

Théo St. Raphaël would ever love her was a ridiculous joke—too preposterous even for a dream!

And I don't care, Carrie told herself fiercely as she looked out the window across the beautiful view. She took another deep breath of the fresh morning air, scented with flowers and sunshine. The colors looked so vivid and brilliant, she thought in wonder. It was as if she'd just woken from a year of sleepwalking through a haze of rain and gray.

Why? Because of this beautiful country? Or because Théo was sleeping in the room down the hall?

She turned away from the window. Going to the *en suite* bathroom, she showered and got dressed in a simple blue sundress. Impatiently combing the tangles from her long brown hair, she stared at herself in the mirror.

"If you're telling me the truth, and Henry is my son, you will soon be my wife."

A year ago she would have wept with joy at such an unromantic proposal. But not anymore. Carrie squared her shoulders. She wasn't going to waste another second wishing for a dream that could never happen. The man she would love someday would be perfect—kind, strong and steadfast.

Nothing like the Count of Castelnau.

And yet as she walked with Théo out of the private medical office in Aix-en-Provence later that day, her heartbeat quickened every time he brushed against her. She couldn't stop looking at him out of the corner of her eye—at the shape of his body in the black T-shirt, snug over his shoulders and biceps, and the dark jeans that fit him far too well. As Théo bent to lift their recently purchased stroller down the stone steps to the crowded street, her gaze traveled over the hard, muscular curve of his backside and her mouth went dry.

Straightening, he looked at her with heavily lidded dark eyes, then gave her a slow-rising smile. "See something you like?"

With a horrified gasp, Carrie looked away sharply. Her cheeks burned as she pretended to be entranced by a nearby jeweler's shop window. "I did, actually. There's a…" She saw a huge diamond ring and her eyes briefly lost focus. "Holy cow, is that thing for real?"

He came closer, pushing the baby stroller, and paused to look down at the diamond ring. "Yes, I believe it is."

Théo was so close she could feel the warmth of his body, and heat flashed through her that had nothing to do with the noontime sun. Their eyes met, and Carrie suddenly lost awareness of the throngs of people crowding past them, shopping in the charming outdoor market in the nearby square. His dark eyes burned through her, black as burning coals. Embers of heat caused memories to rush through her.

"I need you," he'd whispered against her skin as his mouth worshipped every inch of her body in the Seattle hotel. *"I never want to let you go."*

But he *had* let her go. The instant she'd been foolish enough to love him, he'd ruthlessly dropped her.

She couldn't be tempted by his charm again. She *couldn't*.

Tilting his head toward the enormous diamond ring, he gave her a wicked grin. "Care for a souvenir?"

"No, thanks," she said stiffly. She glanced down at the baby in the stroller. "One souvenir from you is enough."

A torturous silence fell between them—a silence filled with memories and regrets. Finally Carrie could bear it no longer.

"So that's it?" she said to break the silence. "That's all we need to do?"

"Just the swab of saliva—yes. The lab computers will compare DNA and we'll soon have the proof if I'm Henry's father. Or not."

His voice was easy, casual, not at all tortured. She looked at him incredulously. Didn't he feel the same agony she felt, being so close? Hadn't he been kept awake last night, as she had? She looked at his face. He looked fresh, rested, impossibly handsome.

Of course he did. Why should having her in his house have any effect on him whatsoever? To him, she was just one woman out of a hundred.

"I never stopped wanting you, Carrie...I have never forgotten how it felt to have you in my bed."

He frowned at her. "*Chérie,* is something wrong?"

"A week here with you just feels so long," she said over the lump in her throat. "I don't know how I'll bear it." Turning away, she started to push the baby stroller forward through the square.

"Carrie. Wait."

She paused, looking back at him. He looked so handsome, taller and more broad-shouldered than any other man in the square. Any man in the world. Time stopped when she looked at him, as if all the people around them were blurs of a Mistral wind and he were the only solid rock, the earth itself.

"What?" she choked out.

Coming close to her, he gave her a smile that lit up his whole face, all the way to his seductive dark eyes. "You must be starving after only toast and jam for breakfast. It was the best I could manage with my housekeeper gone."

"No, it was fine," she stammered. "I loved your toast."

Hearing herself, she bit her lip in chagrin. *I loved your toast?* She sounded like an idiot!

His smile widened. "Let me make it up to you with lunch at a good restaurant, cooked by a proper chef. The place I have in mind has three Michelin stars."

Michelin? she thought blankly. Didn't they make tires? "Fine. Good. Great."

She sounded like a blithering idiot, even to her own ears.

But what did she care what Théo thought about her? she asked herself fiercely. His opinion meant absolutely nothing to her!

But it was getting harder and harder to believe that. It was one thing to hate him at a distance of five thousand miles, something else entirely to maintain her hatred—or even indifference—when he was right in front of her. After a year of dreaming about him, every time she looked up into his cruelly handsome face she felt a shock. Every time she caught his speculative dark eyes on hers, every time she felt the warmth of his body brush against her own, it caused her to shake and melt somewhere deep inside.

"First we need to get some food," he said, nodding down toward the bustling outdoor market in the square. "I'm going to make you dinner tonight, and the cupboard is completely bare."

"What were you planning to do for dinner before?"

"I was going to fly you to Paris and seduce you on the plane, making love to you constantly." Théo looked at her and held her gaze. Awareness sizzled through her before he said with a shrug, "But now that our plans have changed we will stay alone at the castle tonight. Lilley is home in Minnesota, visiting her family." He pulled his phone out of his pocket. "I will tell her to return at once."

Carrie thought of Lilley, Théo's distant cousin who worked as his housekeeper, being forced to return early. She put her hand over his on the phone. "No, don't!"

He looked down at her hand, then tilted his head up with an inscrutable dark gaze. "No?"

Stiffening, Carrie pulled back her hand and tried to laugh. "Any employee of yours deserves all the vacation they can get," she muttered.

Théo barked a laugh. Coming very close, he looked down

at her. "Without my cousin we'll be alone at the castle. Doesn't that make you nervous?"

Her heart stopped in her chest.

"No," she stammered. "Why would I be?"

He leaned forward to whisper, "Because, whether you admit it or not, you know you'll soon be in my bed."

Their eyes met, then their fingertips brushed as they both reached for the handle of the stroller at the same time. Carrie sucked in her breath, ripping her hands away as if he'd burned her.

He took the handle in both his large hands and turned toward the square. "The market is crowded, so stay close," he said casually. "I would hate to lose you."

An hour or so later, after sampling cheeses and fruits and bread across the outdoor market—even once having Théo feed her a piece of chocolate truffle—Carrie was congratulating herself as they left the crowded street with their bags packed beneath the baby stroller. She'd made it through this outing with Théo without making a total fool of herself. Well…mostly.

He turned to her abruptly as they left the market.

"I have something I need to do," he said. "I'll meet you at the Auberge in an hour." He handed her a platinum credit card. "Buy toys for the baby. Clothes for yourself. Gifts for your family. Anything you want."

He was leaving her here—and paying her off with a credit card. She stared down at the card in dismay. "I don't want that."

"Take it." He pushed it into her hand. When she didn't move, he lifted an eyebrow. "Unless you are so enamored of my company you don't want me to leave you—not even for a moment."

Carrie lifted her chin. "Are you kidding? Being without you for sixty whole minutes? It'll be paradise!"

His lips twisted with amusement. "I thought you might feel that way."

She bit her lip. "But where are you going?"

He just gave her an inscrutable smile. "See you in an hour."

Without another word, he turned and left.

Against her will, Carrie watched him go, her eyes lingering on the shape of his body as he disappeared back into the crowd of shoppers. He was so aggravating. How dare he make her laugh? How dare he make her enjoy herself? How dare he make her want to like him again, when hatred was her only defense?

She came back to herself with a start when she heard her baby whine, squirming in his stroller seat. "Sorry about that," she told Henry brightly. "We can go." Straightening, she looked at the credit card in her hand. She tapped the card thoughtfully against her cheek.

So…Théo wanted her to shop, did he?

Théo took the bags out of the back of the SUV and brought them into the main hall at the *château*. He had to make a second trip. He'd never seen so many bags.

"Is that it?" he said finally.

"Yes, I believe so." From the rocking chair by the window, where she was nursing the baby, Carrie gave him a serene smile. "I had the rest of my packages sent directly to the States."

Théo tried not to look toward her full, bare breast, covered only by a blanket. He licked his lips, his eyes looking everywhere but at her breasts, though he could think of nothing else. "What else did you buy?"

She waved her arms expansively. "Gifts for friends and family."

"Gifts?"

She looked at him innocently. "For Christmas."

He stared at her. "It's June."

Her smile was full of mischief. "I bought some bottles of wine to send to my second cousins in Texas, and perfume for friends in Bellevue, and of course my nieces and nephews all needed toys…"

"I hope you didn't leave anyone out," he said pointedly.

Her smile spread to a wicked grin as she pointed toward the small address book peeking out of her purse. "Nope, I didn't. I double-checked."

Théo almost laughed aloud. She looked so pleased with herself—as if she really thought she'd injure him, stiffing him with a high credit card bill. The truth was that he cared little about the fortune he'd amassed over the years. Although spending it certainly had its enjoyable moments, for him money was primarily a way of keeping score in business, of knowing when he'd won. He didn't mind sharing his money…as long as she shared his bed. But he feared it would take far more than money to convince her to be his wife.

It was strange. Usually he did everything he could to convince his mistresses not to love him. He had no experience trying to convince a woman to stay.

But he would. He must.

His hunger for her would soon be satisfied. But seducing her into becoming his mistress was no longer enough. Because of what he'd just learned about the baby, he would make Carrie his wife. By any means necessary.

"I probably spent a thousand dollars today." Carrie looked down with satisfaction at all the piles of brightly colored bags surrounding her on the Turkish carpet. "And in a minute I'm going to use your phone," she added smugly. "It's an overseas call. Likely will cost you a bundle."

He barked an amused laugh. "Go right ahead."

"Now you'll know never to cross me." She looked so

happy, so mischievous, so young. Théo was unable to look away from her beautifully glowing face, her chestnut hair falling in waves down her shoulders. Sitting in the rocking chair near the enormous stone fireplace sculpted with his family's coat of arms, holding their child with such pride and love, Carrie already looked like the Countess he soon would make her.

Coming closer, Théo brushed her hair off her shoulders and said, smiling, "A thousand dollars is nothing. We spent almost that much just on our lunch, with the wine."

She gasped aloud. "A thousand—on lunch?"

"Didn't you enjoy it?"

"Those foamy quail eggs?" she said in shock.

Hmm, he thought. It didn't sound like she'd enjoyed the elegant lunch quite as much as he'd hoped. "I only mean that I want you to enjoy spending my money as you please. It's your money as much as mine. Or it will be once you're my wife."

The light mood between them evaporated. She pulled away from his hand.

"Sorry," she said stiffly. "Not interested."

"I'm not trying to buy you, Carrie," he said, exasperated. "I just want you to be happy here."

Her hazel eyes were cold. "I won't be happy until we leave." She turned away, rising to her feet. "It's time for Henry's nap."

Smooth. Very smooth, he thought, irritated at himself. Where was his usual finesse when he needed it most? He set his jaw. "*Eh, bien,* I'll start making our dinner."

She paused at the hallway, turning back to face him. "And, to answer your question, no. I didn't like the quail eggs. I'm a simple girl. I don't need all that fancy stuff."

"What *do* you need?" he asked quietly.

She paused, and he saw a flash of pain in her eyes. "Something you can never give me."

Théo's hands tightened as he watched her take his son down the hallway.

For Henry *was* his son. There was no longer any question. Théo had gotten the results from the lab two hours after they'd taken the test, when he'd left Carrie alone to shop in the busy town. He'd paid a fortune to get the technicians to drop all their other work and make his test their priority, but it had been worth it.

"The child is your son, Monsieur le Comte," the head technician had told him gravely in his private office, showing him the printed data. "There can be no doubt."

Théo's son. Carrie hadn't lied. She'd tried to tell him the truth many times over a span of months, with messages left on his cell phone and even with his secretary at his office in Paris.

"Théo, please call me. We need to talk."

"When will you be in Seattle again? I have something to tell you."

"Why won't you answer me? Please, Théo, it's important!"

But he'd ignored them all until she'd stopped trying. He'd done his best to forget her, to pretend she didn't exist. And so he'd unknowingly abandoned his own child.

All because he'd been so afraid of Carrie loving him. Well… Théo gave a low, ironic snort. No chance of that now. He would have been grateful for that fact, except she also no longer trusted him. Now it would be difficult to make her believe he could be a decent father. It was a miracle she'd even given him the chance to meet his son. But then, Carrie's kind heart had always been her weakness.

"I'll die before I'll become your wife—paternity test or no."

He set his jaw. Now he knew Henry was his son, there was no way he'd allow her to take the baby back to Seattle, to be raised in a country on the other side of the ocean. There was no way he'd allow some other man to claim Carrie as his wife, to proudly call Henry his son.

A low growl came from the back of his throat. Carrie would be his wife. As of this moment she belonged to Théo and no other man.

But until she accepted that destiny he could not let her know he'd gotten the paternity test results. She'd only agreed to remain in France until he got proof. If Carrie discovered Théo already knew he was Henry's father she'd flag down a car to take her to the nearest airport and take his son with her back to Seattle.

She expected the test results to take about a week. He would use that time to convince her a loveless marriage was the best and only choice for her life, and their son's. Théo would have to execute a full-scale onslaught of seduction to possess her. But he was arrogantly confident he would win.

It was time to be ruthless.

Théo walked down the hall to the large, remodeled kitchen, with its restaurant-grade appliances, all shining stainless steel. He unpacked the fresh ingredients they'd purchased earlier that day from the outdoor market, and with a sardonic twist of his lips pulled on an apron over his black shirt and trousers. Glancing out the window to the garden, he set his jaw. This would work. It *had* to work.

He began to chop carrots against the wood cutting board.

He heard Carrie enter the kitchen. "Where's the—?" Her voice ended with an intake of breath. "What are you doing?"

"Cooking," he said.

"I thought you were joking."

He glanced at her, his eyebrow lifted in cool amusement. "Shocking, isn't it?"

She stared at him for a long moment, then shook her head as if clearing the cobwebs from her mind. "Where's the phone?"

Chopping up steak and putting it to marinate in red wine, he nodded toward his hip pocket. "It's there."

She stared at his hip pocket, then bit her lip. "Um. I'd rather use the house phone."

"I only use my cell at the castle. I'd get the phone for you myself, but…" He showed her his hands, all covered with the marinade he had just made for the beef.

"Fine," she mumbled. Blushing, she reached the barest tips of two fingers into his jeans pocket. As soon as she had his phone in her hand, she exhaled and backed up to the other side of the kitchen.

"Calling your parents?"

"I called them yesterday. If you must know, I'm calling my boss."

Saying nothing, Théo started to chop onions and tomatoes for the *boeuf en daube*. As he added bits of orange peel, fresh thyme and cognac, he heard her call the bayside restaurant in Seattle where they'd first met.

"Hey, Steve?" Her voice was nervous and she paused, biting her lip. "This is Carrie. Um, I won't be able to come to work tomorrow. Really I need the whole week off, if that's all right…?"

Théo heard shouting coming from the other end of the line. Apparently her boss was none too pleased.

Carrie took a deep breath. "I know it's a huge inconvenience for you. I'm so sorry." There was a pleading note in her voice that Théo didn't like one bit. "I'm not in Seattle. I'm in France for a…a family emergency. Please don't fire me. I'll do anything. I'll work two nights for free when I get back." She paused, then took a deep breath. "Okay, all right, a week…"

Guilt and shame ripped through Théo. While he had squandered an extra ten million euros on the steel company in Brazil, for the fleeting satisfaction it gave him, Carrie had been working on her feet for low wages, trying desperately to support their child. He suddenly couldn't handle the pleading, fearful tone of her voice for another second.

His hands shook with fury as he wiped them on the apron. Crossing the kitchen, he ripped the cell phone from her hands.

"Carrie's not coming back. Ever," he said to the unseen boss in cold rage. "Find another waitress. She's too good for you!"

Théo hung up. Tucking the cell phone back in his pocket, he calmly poured olive oil into two cast-iron pans over the gas burner.

"What have you done?" Carrie sounded shocked.

"You're not working there. Not anymore," he replied coolly. He dumped the beef into the larger pan, where it almost immediately began to sizzle. "You never have to work there again."

Her mouth was agape in fury and grief. "He was going to let me have the week off!"

"So you'd work for free when you got back?" His lips set in a grim line. "No."

"You don't know how lucky I was to have that job!"

"Lucky to be on your feet all day and serve salmon platters for four dollars an hour?"

"Ten dollars! When you count tips…"

"You're not going to work anywhere you're not appreciated," he ground out, chopping bacon with more force than necessary and putting it into the smaller pan. "You never have to work again if you don't wish it."

She barked out a laugh. "And just what do you think I should do to earn money? How will Henry and I live?"

He couldn't believe she'd even asked. He glared at her. "I will provide for you both."

She stared at him with her mouth open, then stumbled back a step in the kitchen. "Is that some kind of joke?"

He hadn't expected that.

"Why?" he demanded. "I can afford it."

"You think I would trust you to take care of us?" She drew herself up with furious dignity. "Why would I ever give up myself and my child to your power?"

It was like a knife-blade in his gut.

"You can trust me, Carrie," he ground out. "I never would have left you if I'd known you were pregnant."

"Right. You're not even sure he's your son, or you wouldn't have demanded a paternity test."

"I shouldn't have doubted you," he said in a tight voice.

"So you'll cancel the paternity test?"

In her suddenly hopeful tone of voice he heard her real question: When could she leave?

"You can't leave until the week is through." He set his jaw. "We're going to wait for the official results."

"Of course. You don't just believe I'm telling the truth," she said glumly. She shook her head. "How could I ever trust you to take care of Henry when I know—*I know!*—you don't have the loyalty or commitment necessary to love him forever?"

He glowered at her. "You should know the love of a parent is different from—"

She cut him off. "The only reason I'm even still here is because I know that by the end of this week you'll grow weary of the novelty of a child and give me full custody."

"I won't."

Her eyes glittered. "We both know you don't have what it takes to commit to anyone. Or anything."

He put down the knife. As the meats cooked in the two

pans on the wide eight-burner stainless-steel stove behind them, he stalked toward her. Folding her arms, Carrie stared up at him, clearly nervous but standing her ground.

Inches away, he looked down at her.

"I'm ready to commit to you," he said. "Right now."

"Now?" she taunted. "When you don't even know for sure Henry's your son? I'm probably lying. I'm also clearly stupid and blind—since I once loved *you.*"

Clenching his hands into fists, Théo glared at her. Then, slowly, he exhaled.

"You're not stupid, Carrie. You just believe the best of people. You dream of a world that does not exist."

"Don't worry." Her voice was bitter. "I don't think you're a knight in shining armor anymore."

He took a deep breath, fighting to contain the feelings of guilt and regret that boiled inside him, churning into anger. "I know I treated you badly. But I want to make it up to you. Starting with…this."

Reaching into his pocket, he took out a small velvet jewelry box.

He heard Carrie's intake of breath as he held it out to her. Her eyes fell upon the black velvet box as if it were a poisonous hissing snake. "What is that?"

He pushed it into her hands. "Just open it."

Biting her lip, she slowly opened the box.

The facets of an enormous canary-yellow diamond, surrounded by white diamonds, sparkled in the afternoon sunlight of the kitchen, moving flickers of colored light against her creamy skin.

"What is this?"

"It's the one I saw you looking at in the window of the jewelry shop."

"It's an engagement ring."

"Yes."

She looked up at him, her eyes huge. "That's where you went when you left me in town?" she breathed. "To the jeweler's?"

"The jeweler said it once was part of the dowry of Empress Eugénie," he evaded. "Now it will belong to the new Comtesse de Castelnau." He wrapped his hands over hers. "It will belong to *you*."

Her cold fingers trembled beneath his. He wanted to warm her hands. He wanted to keep her warm and safe forever—to show her he wasn't the man she thought.

Carrie lifted her gaze, and her eyes shone with unshed tears. "Why are you doing this, Théo?" she whispered. "To punish me?"

"Punish you?" With a diamond? His forehead creased. "I want to be a father to my son. I want Henry to have two parents and the security of a real home." He looked straight into her eyes and said in a low voice, "And I want you in my bed, Carrie. I've never stopped wanting you."

She sucked in her breath, searching his gaze. He felt her tremble again, then, with a gasp, she ripped her hands away. Snapping the box shut, she pushed it back into his hands. She looked out the kitchen window, with its bright view of vineyards and sunflowers. "I can't be your mistress. I won't be your wife."

Théo set his jaw. Forcing himself to relax, not to show her how much her words stung, he tucked the jewelry box back in his pocket. He turned away, grabbing an expensive bottle of red Châteauneuf-du-Pape wine he'd brought up from the cellar. Opening the bottle, he poured it into two glasses. He held out a crystal goblet. "Here."

She stared at the glass he held out, then took it. He waited, staring between her and the wine. With a sigh, she took a sip.

"Delicious," she said sadly.

"Better than foamy quail eggs?"

She snorted a laugh. "Anything is better than that."

"Wait until you see what we're having for dinner. Help me cook?"

"*Help* you? In case you haven't noticed, I'm not exactly desperate to spend time with you."

He lifted a dark, sardonic eyebrow. "But, hating me as you do, surely you would not wish me to slave over a hot stove alone? You don't wish to owe me a favor."

She stiffened. "Absolutely not."

He lifted an eyebrow. "So help me." He held out a second apron. When she didn't move, he gave her a wicked half-grin, lifting an eyebrow suggestively. "Unless you're afraid to be close to me…"

"Don't be ridiculous," she bit out. She took a long gulp of wine before she set down the glass. She held out her hand. "Give it here."

But instead of giving her the second apron he reached out and lifted up her hair softly. Putting the apron over her shoulders, he tied the belt around her slender waist. Then he turned her around in his arms to face him. He kept his arms around her waist, her body snug against his in the kitchen as the beef and bacon continued to sizzle on the stove behind them.

Hot desire rushed through Théo like adrenaline as he held her. Her hair felt like cornsilk, her skin soft and smooth as satin. He ached to touch and kiss every inch of her, to rip off her clothes, to stroke and caress and taste her naked skin. He wanted her so badly he shook with it. He wanted to possess her completely and bring her to gasping fulfillment as he plunged himself deeply inside her. He was overwhelmed by the memory of the last time he'd had her in his bed…

He felt her shiver in his arms, and knew she was remembering the same.

She licked her lips, and her wide gaze locked with his. "I

won't let you seduce me, Théo," she choked out. "I won't. I can't."

But he saw the desperation in her eyes, and knew she was speaking the words to try to convince herself they were true. He saw her tremble, saw the hot flush on her skin, saw the way her teeth gnawed at her full, pink bottom lip. And he knew nothing would stop him from having her.

Tonight.

He cupped her chin in his hands.

"Love doesn't last." He looked down at her beautiful face. "But let me show you what we could have in our marriage. Let me show you what you're tossing away. Security. Comfort. Beauty. And passion," he breathed in her ear. "A lifetime of pleasure."

As he pulled away, her eyes flashed up at him in an expression of fear and desire. "No, Théo." Her voice was barely audible, a small cry from the heart. "Please. Don't do this to me…"

But he was beyond mercy. Holding her tight in his arms, he ruthlessly lowered his mouth to hers.

CHAPTER FOUR

HEAVEN. She'd fallen into heaven.

Carrie's eyes closed as she felt his lips, so hot and wet, moving hard against her own, drawing her back into the memory of desire. She felt the roughness of his jawline, like sandpaper against her skin. She felt his hands move against her cheek, her neck, her hair. His body towered over hers, making her feel small and cherished in his powerful arms. She wanted to surrender. But she knew where this kiss would lead. She could not allow it to happen. *Could not—*

"No," she breathed, struggling to pull away.

But he was relentless. His black eyes burned through her. "I'm going to have you, Carrie. In my bed," he whispered. "In my life—forever."

She looked around the kitchen wildly, desperate for a means of escape or, failing that, some protection to cling to. The enormous kitchen was the size of her parents' whole house, like something out of a glossy magazine. The high ceiling had a fresco of eighteenth-century hunting scenes looking down on the brand-new professional-grade appliances. A fire roared in an old brick fireplace beside the gleaming stainless-steel refrigerator. In another life she'd have loved it here...

"I don't love you." She tried to pull away from him, but he wouldn't let her go.

"We're not talking about love. We're talking about desire. I want you, Carrie," he said roughly. "And I know you want me."

She shook her head desperately. "You're wrong—"

For an answer, he kissed her hard and deep, kissed her until she went limp in his arms. Then, to her shock, he picked her up, lifting her against his hard chest.

"I've wanted you for a year," he growled, looking down at her. "I've waited long enough."

Grimly, he started to walk. Dazed, she looked up at his face as he carried her. High over his head, she saw the fresco. She saw a man on a horse, pursuing a deer through the forest. And she knew how her own hunt would end.

He carried her up the sweeping stairs, taking the steps two or three at a time, and with complete inevitability strode into his bedroom. As he set her down gently on the enormous bed, with its black coverlet and black silk sheets, the place where she'd lost her virginity a year ago, she saw the same Spartan, masculine furniture and French doors opening to a wide balcony.

Carrie looked up at him, trembling, terrified. His fierce dark eyes became gentle as he reached down to stroke her cheek. "Are you so afraid?"

The small word choked her. "Yes."

"You have nothing to fear," he said softly.

But how could she explain what she feared most—that if she gave him her body she would once again lose her heart? The last time he'd left her she'd collapsed into a black void from which she'd barely started to recover.

She had a single image through the windows, of vineyards stretching to the cragged mountains beneath blue skies, before Théo lowered himself over her. She had a single deep breath of lavender as a warm summer breeze blew against her skin, then his mouth was on hers and all she could smell was the intoxicating scent of him, luring her with musk and soap and *him*.

She felt the weight of his body over hers as he kissed her deeply, pressing her into the bed. His hands slowly ran through her hair, stroking down her neck. She felt her body tighten as a sigh escaped her lips. She was lost in his kiss. His tongue flicked against hers and he bit at her lower lip, cupping her face with his hands before kissing her more deeply.

His hot mouth caressed down her throat, his tongue darting into the concave hollow of her collarbone. His large hands moved down her body, holding her to the bed as he kissed her bare shoulders. Lifting one of her hands to his lips, he kissed it, his mouth warm against her skin as he looked down at her. Their eyes locked as his dark gaze burned through her.

Turning her hand over, he kissed her palm. She nearly gasped as he slowly suckled each fingertip, his hot tongue sliding into the gaps between her fingers.

Her nipples hardened, and an aching place low in her belly become agonizingly tight. He was repeating the long, languorous caress with her other hand, and she felt the slide of his tongue as he took each fingertip into his hot mouth, sucking gently. A low gasp escaped her.

He sat up, his legs splayed over her thighs, never looking away from her face as he pulled off his black T-shirt. She looked up in wonder. His chest was even more broad-shouldered and hard-muscled than she remembered. A scattering of dark hair stretched between his nipples and his taut, flat belly, pointing down to the waistband of his jeans like an arrow. She swallowed, her eyes wide. She could hardly miss seeing the shape of the enormous hard shaft beneath the dark denim, ready for her...

Sliding his hands down her legs, he pulled up the skirt

of her blue sundress until it was bunched around her hips. He looked down at her simple white bikini panties and his breathing became a gasp. One hand reached for her panties as the other started to undo his fly. Then he froze.

Releasing his grip, he leaned forward and whispered, "I want to take you right now. Push myself all the way inside you in a single thrust."

She trembled.

"But I've waited too long for that." His voice was low, barely audible as she felt the soft movement of his lips against the flesh of her ear. "I'm going to make this worth my year of agony."

He cupped her full, aching breasts through her dress. Plumping up the mounds of flesh, he kissed the skin along the edge of her neckline, moving his heavily muscled body over hers, grinding his hips against her. The secret place between her legs began to ache as it hadn't for a year.

He'd been her only lover, and she still remembered how good it had been between them—how addictive, like sweet poison candy. This was even more explosive than she remembered. She shuddered as he slowly unbuttoned her dress and, pulling it off her body, dropped it to the tile floor, followed by her sandals. She was lying across his enormous bed dressed only in a simple white strapless bra and panties.

"You're so beautiful," he choked out. Using only his fingertips, he stroked down her body, from her collarbone to her belly. Caressing down her legs, he lifted one foot and nibbled gently on the bottom of the arch. Pure sensation shot through her, but before she could move he'd already started stroking back up her body, from the sensitive hollow beneath her knees to her inner thighs, and then, finally, to the mound between her legs.

She gasped, gripping the black silk sheets of the bed. He continued to move up her body. Pressing her full breasts together in the cotton bra, he took a sensual lick of the deep crevice between them. Deftly, he undid the back of her bra, and that, too, was dropped to the floor. He stared down in awe at her huge breasts, full and firm to the touch, cupping them with his hands. "I don't remember this."

"I'm still—nursing," she gasped out.

He exhaled. Lowering his head, he kissed around the nipple of one breast, squeezing it gently. She sucked in her breath, her grip tightening on the sheets as he slowly moved down her body, kissing the length of her bare belly.

His wet, soft mouth slid down her bare hip, moving in a circular path to her upper leg and finally her inner thigh. He was teasing her, she realized, but her breath came in ragged gasps just the same. He pushed at the edge of her panties the tiniest bit, and she felt the warmth of his breath between her legs, at her deepest core. She felt so wet and ready for him. She choked out a moan, shifting her hips, desperate for him to push himself inside her...

Abruptly, he moved away. Sitting on the edge of the bed, he pulled off his jeans, one leg at a time, then his silk boxers. He turned back to face her, his dark eyes glowing in the early-evening shadows. "Look at me, Carrie," he whispered. "See how much I want you."

She sucked in her breath at the sight of his huge, hard, tanned body. She'd thought he had willpower of iron, that he could prolong their tension instead of taking her at his will. But now, looking at him more closely, she could see that he barely held himself in check. His need for her was huge, red and throbbing, and even his hands trembled visibly—as if only the barest thread of control kept him from falling upon her in complete, brutal possession.

Slowly, gently, he reached for her, and she could feel the way his fingertips shook as he touched her. He pulled her white cotton panties down her legs and dropped them to the floor. She realized she was stretched across his bed completely nude. She felt the sway of the mattress beneath her as he moved to the foot of the bed between her legs. She felt the heat of his full gaze upon her.

Nervously, Carrie squeezed her eyes shut. Was he noticing the havoc that pregnancy had wrought upon her body? Would he be disgusted by her wider hips, her softly rounded belly, the stubborn last eight pounds of baby weight that wouldn't budge?

With a low, ragged intake of breath, he stroked down the length of her body.

"Comme tu es belle," he whispered. Leaning over her, he cupped her cheek. "Open your eyes."

Reluctantly, she obeyed. The intent expression on his handsome face was ferocious with need. "I have never wanted any woman as much as I want you," he breathed.

He kissed her hard, his lips almost bruising hers in his unrestrained passion. She felt the fragments of his control starting to slip as he held her down beneath him. She felt the enormous hardness of him between her legs, pressing against her, demanding entrance. Unconsciously she swayed her hips against him, desperate in her sweet agony. With a gasp, he pulled away from her. Ripping his mouth from hers, her fell down her body.

Placing his head between her legs, he pressed her legs apart and took a long, wide taste.

A shock of pleasure ripped through her. She cried out, arching her back, trying to pull away from pleasure so intense it was almost pain. But he held her down with his strong hands and forced her to accept the slow lick of his tongue against her wet core. He played her like an instrument—swirling the tip of his tongue against her hard, aching nub one moment, lapping her with its full width the next. He slipped his tongue an inch inside her, then a fingertip, then two. And all the while she felt his hands stretching her thighs wide as he licked and suckled the most sensitive, secret part of her.

Tension coiled low inside her belly, building and tightening through her body. Her hands gripped the black silk sheets in tight fists as she twisted her hips beneath him. Trying to get closer? Trying to break free? She no longer knew, but the pleasure was too intense. She was afraid she would soon pass out. Afraid that she...

That she...

As if from a distance she heard her voice cry out as her body began to shake with growing bursts of agonizing pleasure. Bracing his arms around her, he moved his hips inside her thighs. She panted, writhing beneath him as she started to lose control, as her vision started to go black.

Sheathing his huge, hard shaft in a condom, he planted himself between her legs. With incredible self-control, he pushed himself only a single inch inside her.

She forgot to breathe. Her cries grew in her own ears, became incessant, became desperate. Words came out of her mouth she almost didn't recognize as her own—words that sounded almost like begging...

Shaking, he pushed himself another inch inside her. She gripped his shoulders, straining for more. His eyes were closed, but she saw beads of sweat on his forehead from the effort to hold himself back.

It was only when he heard her start to swear at him, her fingernails digging into his shoulders, that his eyes flew open. He looked down at her, his gaze dark and hungry, and a growl came from the back of his throat. "Admit you want me."

"I want you," she panted.

With a massive, brutal thrust, he pushed himself inside her, so wide and deep that she gasped in shock. He filled and stretched her to the limit. Pulling back, he thrust again, gripping her shoulders, holding her against the mattress as if to prevent her escape. He thrust again, faster, until he rode her hard and deep. The antique bedframe creaked beneath the violence of his possession, swayed perilously beneath them. As the last vestiges of his self-control frayed, he rode her with increasing intensity, forgetting to be gentle, forgetting everything but blinding, brutal need.

She heard his low, hoarse moan build to a shout as the wooden headboard rattled, pounding against the wall. He impaled her completely, touching her heart, and she screamed as the first waves of new fulfillment washed over her. His low voice joined her in ecstasy, and in that instant of black joy she wept without tears and felt the world crash beneath her.

Afterward, they held each other. She felt the warmth of his body against hers. It could have been moments or hours later when she slowly opened her eyes.

Théo's eyes were still closed as he held her against his naked body, protecting her with his strong arms, caressing her, keeping her close. Carrie started to put her arms around him, only to discover that two fragments of the black silk sheet were still in her hands, ripped by her fists.

Closing her eyes, she dropped the fabric and pressed her cheek against his warm, naked chest. She took a deep breath. It would be so hideously easy to fall in love with him again.

Her eyes flew open. She couldn't love him. He didn't want her love. He was a selfish bastard, foolish enough to believe love was a fantasy. He wanted her to resign herself to a loveless marriage, full of empty luxury.

But she'd just slept with him anyway, risking her heart. Risking everything, since she knew from experience how a condom could fail.

Who was the fool now?

The coverlet fell off her shoulders as she sat up naked in bed.

"Where are you going?" he asked lazily behind her.

"Nowhere," she whispered.

It was just sex, she told herself fiercely. Only sex. Meaningless. But she had a lump in her throat. She'd surrendered Théo everything, knowing that she could not give a man her body without also soon giving him her heart.

No, she told herself. She suddenly felt like crying. *I won't love him again. I can't.*

She felt his dark assessing gaze behind her. Could he read her feelings? Did he know that part of her would always love him? That her supposed hatred was nothing more than a desperate attempt to protect her broken heart?

With a low French curse, Théo suddenly sat up beside her in bed, his black eyes wide. "The dinner!"

"What?"

"I left the steak and bacon frying on the stove!"

He leapt naked from the bed, a horrified expression on his chiseled face.

A sudden laugh rose to Carrie's lips. Then, as he reached for a robe, her eyes traced the exquisitely muscled, tanned body of the man who'd just made love to her—the man who'd fathered her child. And all the laughter fell away from her face as she felt the anguished pang in her heart.

She'd just fallen for him. All over again.

Fifteen minutes later, Théo could tell Carrie was lying, and it made him furious.

"Tell me the truth," he ordered, standing next to the kitchen table. "I can take it."

"Um. It's not as bad as it looks," Carrie offered as she sat, her naked body covered by a white terry-cloth robe. "Really." She took another bite of the charred meat and mushy vegetables in an overcooked burgundy sauce and gulped it down hard. He could almost see it go down her throat. "It's um… not half bad."

"You mean it's *all* bad," Théo said glumly.

Wiping her mouth with a linen napkin, she gave him a cheerful smile. "Still better than raw foamy eggs."

Typical Carrie, Théo thought with irritation. Always trying to make the best of things. Dipping his wooden spoon in the congealed sauce, he tasted it and nearly spat it out. Covering his face with his hand, he leaned against the table and groaned. "I wanted to impress you."

Their eyes met. The smile fled from her face.

"You did," she whispered.

An undercurrent of heat passed between them. Suddenly Théo no longer cared about the ruined dinner. The spoon dropped from his hands, clattering to the floor. Pulling her into his arms, he kissed her.

Already he wanted her again.

The kiss lasted a long time before he finally found the strength to pull away.

If once he'd been preoccupied, now he was obsessed.

Their bond would be permanent and strong. He would help Carrie lose her foolish illusions—much as he'd acquire a troubled company and break apart its bankrupt assets, to get a better price for the whole. He would protect the parts of Carrie's soul he admired—her passion, her intelligence, her love for their son. Her kind heart. Her hopeful, tender soul.

But he would help her discard her big dreams, her impossibly romantic ideals. Everything that could not last. Everything she was better off without.

Yes, their marriage would be solid. Their family would be strong.

And he could hardly wait to start on the honeymoon.

Never breaking his gaze from hers, he sat down heavily

in a nearby chair, pulling her into his lap. Wrapping his arms around her, he took her hands in his own. Her hands fell small, delicate and warm. He felt like a clod beside her. She would make the perfect countess.

"We will have a good partnership," he said quietly. "You will be an asset to my life, and I will strive to be an asset to yours."

Twisting around to face him, she looked at him with shock. "What are you talking about?"

"Our marriage." His hands tightened over hers. "We've already started on the honeymoon. We should wed immediately. French law requires a ten-day wait, so I thought perhaps Las Vegas…"

Carrie held up her hand sharply. "You're already planning our wedding?"

Her tone was angry. Of course, Théo thought, biting his lip in chagrin. Every woman wanted to plan her own wedding.

"It doesn't have to be Las Vegas," he said, more carefully. "We could marry in Seattle, so your family could attend. And of course if you feel you want a large, lavish reception I would be more than happy to throw an enormous party afterward, either here in the castle or in Paris. We'd invite all the highest society of Europe. We could have your dress specially made…"

"I'm not going to marry you," she said coldly, "just because we had sex."

"What?" he gasped. His eyebrows lowered. "Of course that's not the only reason. But you felt how perfect we are together—made for each other!"

"Made for each other *in bed*," she said. "A one-night stand changes nothing. You don't want love. I won't marry without it. We'd only make each other unhappy."

He cupped her cheek, looking up at her with a growl. "You didn't seem unhappy a few minutes ago."

She jumped up from his lap. "You're taunting me for wanting you? Fine." Her voice was small as she looked down at her hands. "I wanted you. But that doesn't change my feelings."

"You don't hate me," he persisted, rising to his feet.

For a moment they stared at each other in the darkened kitchen.

"I don't hate you," she agreed sadly. Her eyes were luminous in the shadows of the kitchen's flickering fireplace as she said bitterly, "But I wish to God I did."

He shook his head. "But why? You must know that our marriage would be best for our son."

"It would be a disaster," she said sharply, "when I know you will soon lose interest in being tied down by the ball and chain of a family. Better you abandon us now rather than later, when Henry is old enough to be hurt by it." She lifted her chin. "Nor are you the role model I want for my son as he grows into a man!"

That stung. He stiffened with an intake of breath. "I'm not going to let you take my son from me, Carrie," he said coldly. "You will marry me, whether you wish it or no."

He saw her tremble. "Théo, be reasonable—"

"I will never let you go," he bit out. "Accept that fact. Accept your fate."

He looked down at her plate, at the lavish gourmet meal he'd tried to make that was now burned and inedible. He'd made a mess of dinner, just like his attempt to seduce her into marriage.

But he'd never thought it would be so hard. Angrily, he raked his hand through the back of his hair. How was it possible that the one woman he desired to marry was the only woman on earth who did not wish to marry *him*?

Carrie cleared her throat, and when she spoke, the tone of her voice had changed—as if she were deliberately trying to lighten the mood. "It's been strange to have you serve me a meal," she said softly. She smiled, and her eyes were endless pools of light in the flickering shadows. "Do you remember how we first met?"

He nodded. "I'd never seen any woman so beautiful," he whispered. "I was mesmerized. I couldn't take my eyes off you as you served our table." He grinned. "And then you found out I'd just come from Paris, and you dumped half my food in my lap."

"It was an accident!" she protested. She sighed. "You know I've always dreamed of seeing Paris. The Eiffel Tower, the charming little cafés, everything…" She looked down at her hands. "Someday I'll see the City of Light. Someday."

As he looked at her wistful face, a sudden jarring memory passed through Théo's brain, like the echo of a whisper. It was possible that during their whirlwind affair he might have promised to take her to Paris. In Théo's opinion, promises made in bed were widely considered not to be real vows—just fantasies used to heighten the pleasure. And yet he felt a certain regret looking down at her. Twice now he had brought Carrie all the way to the South of France, and yet she'd still never seen Paris—the headquarters of his company, only three hours by high-speed train, or less by private jet.

Pushing the uncomfortable thought away, he forced out a laugh. "Whatever the reason, you dropped a whole plate of food in my lap when I was in negotiation with my Japanese associates. Face it. Waitressing is not your true gift, *chérie*."

"Yes. Well…" Her face fell even further. "I don't need to worry about that now, since I have no job."

He stared at her unhappy face and felt it again—that annoying pang of guilt. He tried to shrug it away. With his fortune, after they were married Carrie would never need to work again. But, looking at her eyes, he wondered suddenly if she'd had some childhood ambition. Strange that in their time together last year he'd never asked her. But then, during their brief affair they'd rarely managed to spend much time out of bed.

Taking her hand in his own, he leaned forward across the table. "What do you want to do?"

She lifted her eyes. "What will I do?" Her voice was listless. "Find another waitressing job, I suppose."

"I don't want to hear about *jobs*," he said. "What is your dream?"

"Dream?" She frowned, as if he'd just spoken in a language utterly foreign to her.

Ironic, he thought, when Carrie Powell was the most dreamy, idealistic woman he'd ever met. How funny that he'd have to spell it out for her.

"When you were a child," he said, "what did you want to be?"

"Oh." She took a deep breath and her cheeks turned pink. "I never had a dream—not like that. Not really."

"That can't be true."

"It is," she fired back, then faltered. "Well, except…"

"Except?"

"Forget it. You'd just laugh at me."

He leaned across the table. "Try me."

She looked down at his hand over hers, then with an intake of breath she met his gaze. "All my friends dreamed of being doctors, teachers, lawyers. But not me. Ever since I was young there was only one thing I wanted to be."

"What?"

"A wife. A mother." With a strangled laugh, she tossed her head defiantly. "Go ahead and laugh. It's pathetic, right?

A woman in this day and age who just dreams of raising a family and taking care of the people she loves?"

"I'm not laughing," he said quietly.

She still glared at him, clearly waiting for him to mock her. When he did not, she sank back into her chair, putting her head in her hands. "It doesn't matter. I'll find another waitressing job. Or maybe go back to school and train for something that will let me buy a little house of my own someday…"

Her voice trailed off.

"Let me give you your dream," he said. "Let me help keep your family safe and secure—"

"You mean the family that you threatened, so you could blackmail me into staying here?"

He shook his head. "You will be a countess. With all my fortune at your command."

She looked around the kitchen, from the elegant hardwood floor to the old paintings on the high ceilings above, flickering in the firelight of the eighteenth-century brick fireplace.

"You do live well," she said ruefully. She rubbed the back of her head, and her dark hair seemed to cascade down her shoulders like chestnut silk. She looked up at him. "But the only rich family is one that is filled with love."

A low ache settled at the base of his throat. "That sounds nice." Turning away, he picked up his glass of wine from the counter. "Whatever love my parents once had for each other was long gone by the time I was eight. They often forgot me for days on end when they fought—or else they tried to use me as a weapon against each other. It was a relief when they finally divorced."

"I'm so sorry," Carrie said.

But he didn't want her pity. "For the sake of *love*," he said acidly, "my father left my mother to date girls half his age.

For the sake of *love*, my mother has married four times and had children by three different men."

Carrie shook her head. "No wonder you want a loveless marriage," she whispered. "You have no idea what true love even is."

He stiffened. "I know what it is. Illusion. Infatuation. People think marriage will make those feelings last. But it's tricky magic. The harder you try to hold on to it, the quicker it will end. Love always ends. And it usually ends badly."

"But—"

"Did you know that in many Asian cultures white is the color of grieving? The color worn to a funeral?" he interrupted. "A wedding is celebrated as the beginning of love." He looked away. "In truth, it is the end."

"So why did you ask me to marry you, then?" Her voice sounded sodden. "If you think marriage is so awful?"

He looked at her sharply. "I'm not against marriage."

"But you just said—"

"I'm against marrying for the sake of romantic delusion," he said. "Marriage can be the foundation of a solid home, when done right. It's a friendship. A partnership. The start of a family."

"Without love?"

He shrugged. "Without heartbreak."

For a long moment silence fell across the shadowy kitchen. Carrie raised her chin.

"Let me tell you about the kind of marriage that I believe in. A partnership—yes. But not based on mutual goals, as if we were entering into some kind of business arrangement."

"But that's exactly what a good marriage is. A business. Complete with a leadership board and a financial strategy and five-year goals. The company's mission is raising children, ensuring the good of the household and the continuance of the family's existence."

She stared at him incredulously. "But the basis has to be love, or what's the point?"

He looked at her. "Did loving me make you happy?"

Her mouth had been open to speak. She snapped it shut.

"Romantic infatuation brings ruin," he said quietly. "You of all people should know that. Do it my way, Carrie. Just marry me now, without the delusion of romance, and all your grief and stress will melt away. And Henry will always be safe and happy, loved by both of his parents."

She stared at him with an intake of breath, and for an instant he thought she would agree. Then she stood up quickly, swaying on her feet. Her cheeks were red, her hands balled into fists.

"I will never accept your devil's bargain."

Disappointment filled him, crashing down his hopes. He rose to his feet, looking down at her in the dying firelight. "I'm not going to allow my child to be raised by another man, Carrie. Accept this."

"But you still don't know if Henry is even—"

"One of us is going to win this argument." His dark eyes ripped through hers as he leaned forward. "And one of us," he whispered, "is going to lose."

CHAPTER FIVE

CARRIE awoke to the sound of her baby crying. The light of dawn flooded the room as she covered her face with a pillow, yearning for one more moment of sleep.

Then the mattress swayed beneath her. She heard a heavy footstep, and the sobs abruptly stopped with a hiccup.

That alarmed her as nothing else could. She instantly sat up, her pillow dropping softly to her lap.

Théo, shirtless and wearing only drawstring pajama bottoms slung low on his hips, was cradling their son against his bare, hard-muscled chest, crooning softly to the baby in the warm light of morning.

The baby's chubby face peered up at him with a frown. Then, as Théo sang, rocking him in his arms, Henry's face lit up. Théo's deep masculine laughter provided a low baritone counterpoint to his son's baby giggles.

For Carrie, the sound was sweet misery.

The past five days had been full of so many small joys. The three of them had enjoyed playing outside, eating a picnic lunch in the garden beside the stone fountain, lying out amid the sunshine and scent of flowers beneath the wide blue sky.

Small joys. And endless pleasures. Always she felt Théo's dark, smoldering eyes upon her, his hot gaze promising a world of delights the moment their son was asleep in his crib.

Every instant they spent together Carrie was so stretched with awareness she could barely take a deep breath. Shivers filled her body every time she felt his eyes upon her, every time his fingers brushed hers as they held their child between them. She'd given up trying to resist his seduction. Every night they spent together in bed was a revelation as he held and stroked every inch of her body, making her feel beautiful and new. Making her feel she might die from wanting him. *From loving him.*

She'd felt happy.

Too happy.

Thank heaven for his housekeeper, Lilley Smith. The plump, plain young housekeeper, who'd returned three days ago from her vacation, looked nothing like her distant cousin Théo. At twenty-three, she had light brown hair and brown eyes, was motherly and kind, and best of all she adored babies almost as much as they adored her.

If not for Lilley bustling around the castle, tidying the baby's toys behind them or racing to fold laundry or bring out the picnic basket, who knew what insanity might have occurred.

Actually, Carrie knew exactly what would have happened. Sometime when she and Théo were just sitting outside with the baby, lying on a blanket beneath the warm summer sun and feeling the hot breeze blow through the sunflowers and vineyards, she would have broken the silence in the most disastrous way possible—by blurting out that she'd fallen back in love with him.

There could no longer be any doubt. Even when she'd hated him she'd never stopped loving him completely. Now, passion and longing infused her whole being, practically shining like light out of her fingertips and toes. *She loved him.*

Carrie's heart turned over in her chest as she watched

Théo, so masculine and powerful, carefully holding the tiny baby in his footsie pajamas. Henry was beaming up at Théo as father and son smiled at each other. And she watched it with a sinking feeling in her chest. She'd been stupid enough to fall in love with Théo. How could she?

If he found out, he would leave her. And worse: he would leave their baby.

Once, that would have been exactly what she wanted. But not anymore. Not now that she saw the father-son bond growing every day. Was it possible she'd been wrong about Théo? Could he truly be a good husband and father, as long as she played by his rules?

The thought was like a razor blade as Théo moved toward her, leaning to kiss the top of her head in the early-morning light. She felt that tender kiss all over her body.

"Bonjour, chérie," he said softly.

"Good morning," she whispered miserably.

The baby heard her voice and immediately turned to her with a whimper and whine. Théo grinned. "I think he's hungry. He's a growing boy."

The pride in his voice made a laugh escape Carrie in spite of herself. Sitting up straight against the pillow, she reached out her hands. "Give him here."

Théo handed the baby to her where she sat on the bed in her oversize T-shirt. She was making no effort to be pretty this time. She wasn't trying to impress him anymore, as she had last year with sexy clothes and elaborate hair and makeup. This time it was strictly casual, with no makeup, sundresses by day and ratty old T-shirts by night. And yet he seemed dazzled, intoxicated by her. Just as she was by him.

As Carrie started to nurse the baby Théo watched for an instant. His black eyes seemed to devour her. Then he abruptly turned away. "I'll be right back."

Some of the warmth drained out of the room with him. A sigh escaped her lips as Carrie stared after him.

With Théo around there was no such color as gray. He brought vibrancy to her life. He'd taken her from a drizzly life of clouds and rain and made her whole world a summer in Provence, with blue skies, and lavender waving in the hot wind beneath a yellow sun. After a year of winter, she'd opened to him like a sunflower in spring.

She looked down at her blissfully suckling child.

Only two days until they'd get the results of the paternity test, and they could leave. Two more days to keep silent about her feelings.

If she could hide her love for two more days, she and Théo might come to an arrangement. Henry would live with her in Seattle, but often visit his father in France, or Théo would come visit them. And somehow, eventually, when she didn't have to see Théo every single day, her love for him would slowly die.

It was her only hope.

She heard a noise and looked up to see Théo in the doorway. Her eyes unwillingly traced the hard curves of his upper body, his wide shoulders, thickly muscled biceps and flat belly. Even the way he walked toward her caused a sensual shiver across her body.

He set down a breakfast tray near her on the bed. "Your breakfast, milady."

She saw orange juice, coffee with cream, fresh fruit, toast and jam, and an assortment of breads and buttery French pastries. His kindness took her breath away. "You made breakfast?"

He gave her a crooked half grin. "Lilley made it."

"Of course." Carrie smiled up at him, still grateful for the thoughtful gesture, then looked back at the luscious tray.

"I should have known it wasn't you," she teased. "It's not burned black."

He sat down beside her on the bed. His dark, half-lidded eyes seared through her. "I would burn toast for you every morning if that would win you, Carrie," he said in a low voice. "I'd burn it morning, noon and night."

Her heart thudded in her throat, but she tried to smile. "Sorry," she said, trying to keep her voice light. "The ability to burn toast is not the top item on my list for a prospective husband."

"So what is?" he asked, stroking back a tendril of her hair. He leaned forward, his eyes intent. "Tell me how to win you," he whispered against her skin, and she shivered. "Tell me."

Carrie closed her eyes. *Love me. Just love me.*

But she shook her head over the lump in her throat. "Forget it. I'm not going to lose this battle."

He looked down at her. "We'll see."

A shudder went through her. She had to resist. Her fingers gripped the top of the white quilt. She *had* to!

Théo looked down at the baby's downy head with a tenderness that made her heart leap to her throat. "Is he finished?"

The baby had unlatched, and now pushed his head away from her breast. "I think so," she said drily.

Picking him up, Théo cradled his son in his arms. "I'm going to teach you everything," he told the baby. "How to play football, how to ride a bike…"

"How to buy a company and break it up for parts?" she teased.

Théo flashed her a sudden grin, and the way his smile lit up his darkly handsome face took her breath away. *"Ben, oui."*

Still smiling, he sat down on the handwoven rug, holding

the baby in his lap. Putting his large hands over his son's feet, he played a French version of patty-cake, clapping Henry's little feet together lightly. They were quite the pair—Théo so muscular and powerful, sitting bare-chested in pajama bottoms, with their tiny son cradled in his arms. A moment later, he was reading to Henry in French from a picture book about Babar the Elephant that she'd purchased from a bookshop earlier that week. Carrie drank creamy coffee and watched them as she ate pastries in bed, as a beam of golden sunlight hit against the bare skin of Théo's muscular back.

And she wanted him. Wanted *this*. Forever.

The dream she ached for with every cell in her body and every longing of her heart felt more true than reality. She wanted the three of them to be a family.

But Théo didn't love them. Correction: he didn't love *her*. Carrie looked down at her breakfast tray. She couldn't accept a life permanently without love, a marriage that was more like a business than a romantic blending of hearts and souls. She couldn't! Especially when she knew he would soon tire of being a husband and father.

But would he? She'd thought he'd be fed up with them days ago. Instead, his attention to her and affection for Henry had only seemed to grow.

"We'll leave you to have your breakfast, *ma belle*."

She looked up to discover Théo had risen to his feet, cradling their baby against his tanned, muscular chest.

"What? Why?" she blurted out. "You don't have to leave!"

"Enjoy some peace and quiet," he said, smiling down at her. "Have a peaceful breakfast. Take a long shower. Have some time to yourself—as much as you need. Come downstairs when you're ready to start the day. We have a busy day planned." He grinned down at the baby. "Now, let's go downstairs so you can say good morning to Lilley, shall we, *mon petit*?"

"A busy day today?" she called after him. "What do you mean?"

But he didn't stop to answer. She took another bite of almond croissant and looked around her bedroom. It was beautiful, with clean lines and a lovely view from the window. A gauzy canopy hung from the wrought-iron bed frame. But, best of all, when she grabbed the pillow beside hers she could still smell the musky, clean scent of him...

Exhaling, she turned from the pillow. She took a last bite of croissant, then stopped chewing as she stared out blankly toward the windows showing wide fields of sunflowers.

If Théo could truly be a good father, if he wouldn't ultimately tire of having a family and a home and toss them aside to become a globetrotting workaholic again, she had no choice but to marry him. Any decent mother would sacrifice her own life in an instant for a stable home for her child. She had to put her heart on ice. For Henry's sake.

For Henry's sake. Carrie scoffed a laugh at her own soul's sly treachery. It wasn't just for her baby's sake, but her own. She was finding it almost impossible to imagine living without Théo now. She wanted to be his wife, to sleep in his bed every night. She wanted it more than anything.

But how could she accept Théo's terms and be in a loveless marriage for life? How could she bury her love for Théo deep inside her soul, so deep that he would never suspect?

It wasn't in Carrie's nature to keep a secret. She had no talent for lying. Especially since every moment her love for him tortured her, begging for release.

If she married Théo and he discovered she'd once again broken his only rule, he would despise her. It could only end in despair. Even if Théo remained in their marriage, his manner toward her would always be distant, or worse—full of pity.

Was that the home she wanted for Henry? Caught between a cold, rejecting father and a weeping, broken-hearted mother?

No matter how much she yearned to be Théo's wife, she could not surrender to her desire. Or to his constant, unrelenting pursuit.

Pushing her breakfast tray aside, she rose from the bed and crossed the cool tile floor to the en suite bathroom. She took a long, hot shower and closed her eyes, lost in thought and grief. Coming out of the steamy shower, her skin all flushed and pink, she hesitated over the clothes in her closet, then selected a simple sundress.

She brushed her hair, allowing the dark waves to tumble over her shoulders to dry in the warm air. She took her time—a novelty she hadn't enjoyed since her baby was born. She took a whole hour to herself, procrastinating as long as possible before she finally left her bedroom, squaring her shoulders and repeating to herself, *I do not love him. I do not love him.*

Coming down the sweeping stairs, she saw Lilley disappearing into the main hallway of the *château*, singing a children's song in her sweet, slightly off-tune voice to the baby cuddled in one arm, while carrying folded towels in the other. Carrie smiled and opened her mouth to call out.

Then she saw Théo at the bottom of the stairs.

He was pacing, talking on the phone in rapid French. He'd showered and was now dressed in a dark silk button-down shirt and black trousers. He looked sophisticated, sexy. He looked…completely out of her league.

Suddenly she wished she'd made a little more effort. Put on lipstick. A push-up bra. Gotten a new wardrobe and magically lost ten pounds.

Their eyes met, and as he gave her a hot, dark smile a sensual shiver ran through her body. He ended the call and came to her at the base of the stairs. Reaching for her hand, he kissed it.

She smiled at him, then bit her lip. "Why are you dressed like that?"

His dark eyes seared through her. "I'm taking you out."

"Out?" She came slowly down the last steps with a nervous laugh. "Out where?"

"Paris."

She stopped with an intake of breath.

Paris. The city of lovers. The city of dreams. The City of Light.

As a teenager she'd had a picture of the Eiffel Tower that she'd ripped from a magazine on her wall—an image showing the rooftops of the city at the violet hour of dusk. She'd never stopped dreaming of seeing it for real, even when she'd grown older and the dreams had started to seem unlikely.

"Just—just the two of us?" she said hesitantly.

He gave her a single, sensual nod.

"But I couldn't leave the baby—"

"Just for a few hours." He leaned against the smooth wood of the banister, looking casual and debonair. "We'll be back before dinner," he promised.

Her heart pounded in her chest. She couldn't possibly go to *Paris*. It was too dangerous by half. Between Théo's desire for her and her own wanton dreams of them being a family she would find herself in a white dress in no time flat. And then her baby would be the one to suffer for the inevitable, painful, slow failure of their marriage.

She shook her head. "No. We're going to wait here for the results of the paternity test tomorrow. Then I can go home.…"

The expression on his face became dark. Gone was the playful father who'd held their baby so tenderly in his arms.

In this moment he looked hard and ruthless, like the corporate raider he was. "You *are* home."

"Théo—"

"We're leaving in ten minutes for the airport," he said shortly. "We'll be there and back on my jet in a matter of hours." He moved closer, and his eyes seemed to go right through her soul as he said softly, "Don't you want your childhood dream?"

Yes. A million times yes. Carrie forced herself to shake her head. "I don't have time."

"There's always time for dreams," he said quietly. He took her hand. "I want to make them all come true."

But there was only one dream she really needed. For him to love her. She closed her eyes, the truth hovering on her lips. If she told him she loved him, this all would end. He would stop asking her to be his bride. He would kick her to the curb, as he'd done before.

But would he also desert Henry?

"If we go to Paris," he said, "we can go directly to the main lab and find out the results of our paternity test a day early."

Her eyes flew open as she sucked in her breath.

A day early. That could save her—save everything!

One day less to hide her feelings. If she could get out of France without Théo discovering she loved him, he might still stay in Henry's life. They could share custody—at a distance. Henry would have two parents to care for him. And Théo wouldn't be miserable in their marriage, trapped by her love.

Carrie took a deep breath. She could feel the tears behind her eyelids as she surrendered to her only hope. "All right," she whispered. "Paris."

* * *

"There can be no doubt, Monsieur le Comte. This child is your son."

The head of the main Paris branch of the lab spoke gravely, acting as if he expected this news to come as a surprise to Théo. Just as Théo had arranged earlier on the phone.

Feeling Carrie's anxious gaze upon him in the white-walled office in the fifteenth *arrondissement*, Théo widened his eyes, as if it were news he hadn't already heard. With a satisfied sigh, he pulled Carrie into his arms.

"I knew you wouldn't lie to me," he whispered in her ear. "I knew Henry was my son."

Théo felt her shiver in his arms. Shivering with relief? Or something else?

As she pulled away, her hazel eyes were dark with a hidden mystery he couldn't solve. He no longer knew how to win her. And so out of desperation, he'd brought her to Paris.

He could not understand why she continued to resist his proposal. He knew she no longer loved him—she'd stopped loving him long ago. So why did she refuse?

Théo had promised her she could take Henry back to Seattle once they had the results of the paternity test. His time was almost out. Only one day left. After almost a week together he hadn't been able to convince her, in spite of his best efforts both in bed and out of it. He felt frustrated to no end. Didn't she see how good it was between them? Didn't she see how necessary it was for their son's future happiness?

Last night, while he'd been holding her in bed after making love to her for two hours, a devious whisper had crawled through his brain. What if he lied and said he'd fallen in love with her, in that theatrical, fantasy-land, can't-live-without-you way she wanted? Would that lure her at last?

But he couldn't do it. A marriage based on lies was even worse than one based on emotion. And, more than that, he respected Carrie too much to lie to her. She would marry him with clear eyes, or not at all.

So he'd placed all his bets on one roll of the dice by taking her to Paris, to the city of her dreams. He intended to show her, once and for all, what it would mean to live as his countess.

They left the lab and he held open the Ferrari door for Carrie, then drove them into the center of the city. The wind blew against his face and hair in the convertible, even in the slow traffic down the Boulevard Saint-Michel, and the sun felt warm against his face.

He spent hours showing her the sights of the city, including a private tour that whisked them to the top of the Eiffel Tower with all of Paris at her feet. They visited the Arc de Triomphe and then skipped all the queues at the Louvre for a short private tour led personally by a museum curator. Théo had intended next to shower her with jewels and gowns in the exclusive shops of the Champs-Élysées, but when Carrie suddenly sighed and said she would kill for a snack, he shook his head with a laugh. "I know just the place."

Carrie leaned against his shoulder as he drove, and his body tightened. As he drove toward the Ile St. Louis he couldn't stop giving her little glances out of the corner of his eye. As he changed gears his hand brushed her knee. He felt her shiver, heard her intake of breath.

And he suddenly knew he couldn't give her up. Not for honor. Not for anything.

She wasn't leaving this city without agreeing to be his bride.

He pulled the low-slung sports car in front of a tiny, hole-in-the-wall restaurant on a winding street on the Ile St.

Louis—one of the two tiny islands on the Seine in the center of Paris.

"Why are we stopping?" she asked, looking around at the slender streets.

He smiled down at her as a valet hurried around the car. "Lunch."

"Oh, no," she groaned. "Not more foamy quail eggs."

"Don't worry," he said softly. "I know you better than that now."

Handing his car keys to the valet, he came around to the passenger side and helped her out of the car. He touched her hand and didn't want to let go. Once inside, they were guided to the most romantic table at the intimate, cozy restaurant, in a shadowy corner near the medieval fireplace. He held her hand across the table. It was as if they'd gone back in time, he thought, looking at her beautiful face in wonder. As if they were the only two people in the world.

They ordered the prix-fixe menu for fifty euros. It started with *céleri rémoulade*, was followed by coq au vin, all washed down with the house red. For dessert he chose a platter of cheeses, while Carrie had crème brûlée. And all throughout the delicious, intimate meal, in the dark, low-ceilinged old restaurant, he asked her questions.

As she spoke, he couldn't take his eyes off her. The sound of her voice was like music. His sexy lover. The angelic mother of his child. Her lustrous skin was the color of cream in winter, and her chestnut hair cascaded in waves down her bare shoulders. Her laughter was the sound of bells. He felt lost in her in a way he didn't understand, in a way he'd never felt before.

He couldn't lose her. Not now.

Not ever.

Carrie was chattering easily, on her second glass of wine. Her cheeks had turned pink as roses. "This is the most delicious meal I've ever had." She held up the glass. "To you knowing what I like."

He grinned. After clinking glasses, they both drank deeply. "And to our son," he said, lifting his glass a second time.

"Oh, that's even better! Yes! To Henry."

They both drank, and he leaned across the table to refill her glass. They smiled at each other across the table, the mood warm and happy, and with some other emotion he couldn't quite understand. But it was now, he thought, or never.

With a deep breath, he pulled the black velvet box out of his pocket. He placed it on the small table beside the empty ceramic bowl that had once held crème brulée.

"This is the last time I'm going to ask, Carrie," he said huskily. "Will you marry me?"

The color in her cheeks turned pale as she stared at the huge canary-yellow diamond surrounded by white diamonds, set in platinum. She lifted her chin, and her eyes glittered with unshed tears.

"I can't."

"Why?" he demanded.

She looked up at him miserably. "If we ever really needed you...if we ever really—" she took a deep dragging breath "—*loved* you, you would leave us."

His eyes darkened in a scowl. "I am getting a little tired of you always accusing me of this."

"Am I wrong?"

"The love between parent and child is sacred. It lasts. It's different from the romantic foolishness you dream about."

She set her jaw. "How long would Henry and I stay with you in the castle before you grew weary of our devotion and left us?"

"This isn't about Henry. You know I would never leave

him now. This is about *you*," he said harshly. "And how you're selfishly putting your own romantic dreams ahead of what's best for our child."

"I'm not!" she cried. "Us getting married would be a disaster for everyone—especially him!"

"How can you say that?"

"Don't you see?" She took another deep breath. He saw her fingers gripping the edge of the table as if she were clinging on for dear life. "Living apart, sharing custody of our son while we live on opposite sides of the world, is his only hope for a happy life."

He stared at her. "You're making no sense!"

She pressed her lips together, her face pale. "Once we were married you'd treat me badly. Our home would become a misery."

"How can you say that?" he ground out. "I will never treat you badly! I respect you—care for you! Don't you know that by now?"

She started to say something, then choked herself off, midbreath. She looked away, looking across the shadows of the medieval setting. "I could say something that would make you go away."

"No." He grabbed her hand across the table. Her fingers were shaking and cold to the touch. He pressed her hand against the warmth of his cheek. Turning her hand over, he kissed her naked palm. "We'd be equal partners. Friends. Parents. There's nothing you could say to drive me away."

Licking her heart-shaped lips, she took a deep breath. Then she looked at him with eyes full of pain.

"I'm in love with you," she whispered.

For a second Théo thought he hadn't heard her right. He must have misunderstood. She couldn't be *in love* with him. He held his breath, searching her eyes. She looked pale, like she might faint.

"You—love me?" he said finally.

Miserably, she nodded. "I can't resist you. Not anymore," she said in a low voice. "And this is the only way to make you understand. You would despise me. And I would feel…like my heart was ripped out." She gave a tearful laugh. "Better this ends now. We'll separate and share custody. Henry will always feel loved by both of us. You will be free. And I…"

"And you what?" he said sharply.

Blinking back tears, she tried to smile as she looked at him. "I can at least live in hope."

"For another man to love you?"

Her voice was almost too quiet for him to hear. "Yes."

Théo looked away. He thought of his son being shuttled back and forth between America and France, as he had been. He thought of his son being raised with stepparents and half-siblings, never quite feeling like he fully belonged anywhere. Some other man would raise his son at least half the year.

And every night that same man would have Carrie in his bed.

Rage ripped through him. He would die before he'd allow Carrie to be loved by another.

"I tried to hate you," she whispered, leaning her head on her hand. "I tried so hard. But I can't stop myself from loving you." She looked up suddenly. "Don't punish Henry for my weakness," she pleaded. "We'll find a way for you to spend time with him, but never have to see me again—"

"No," he bit out, gripping his hands into fists.

Tears spilled unheeded down her cheeks. "Don't do this, Théo. I know you must despise me, but Henry is an innocent child—"

"I'm not going to let you go." Reaching across the table, he cupped her face and looked down into her eyes fiercely. "You *will* be my wife."

"But, Théo," she choked out, shaking her head, "it's im-

possible. I can't love you desperately while you feel nothing—"

"You're wrong," he bit out, and then, with a deep breath,
he forced out the lie he had no choice but to tell. "I love you,
too."

Incredulous, slow-rising joy lit up her beautiful face, like
golden dawn across fields of red poppies. "You—love me?"

"Yes," he ground out.

Trembling, she closed her eyes. Then, bursting into tears,
she stood up and reached across the table, throwing her arms
around him with a heartfelt sob that made all the other pa-
trons of the small restaurant turn their way.

He'd made her deliriously happy with his lie. He could
hear it in her tears. He could feel it in the way her soft, cur-
vaceous body swayed against his as she clutched him tightly,
as if she never wanted to let him go.

"We're engaged," he announced grimly to the other
diners, and there was a breathless *awwwww*, a scattering of
applause.

Paris was the legendary City of Light. A city for lovers.
And he'd ruthlessly used her dreams against her.

After her year of heartbreak and grief she truly believed
all her romantic hopes had come true. And even though part
of him recoiled at the lie he'd just told, he couldn't quite
regret it. Because he'd won. Now he could keep her forever.

Even if it meant he'd lost his soul.

"Come on," Théo said roughly, grabbing her hand. "Let's
get you a wedding dress."

CHAPTER SIX

By THE next morning, Théo was starting to fear that he was going to lose far more than his soul.

After he'd gotten the enormous diamond on her finger, he'd driven her straight to the most expensive bridal shop on the Avenue Montaigne and bought the first wedding dress that Carrie adored. Then he'd driven her immediately to the airport.

They'd made love four times since then—once on the jet, three times more since they'd arrived back at the *château*—and he was amazed at the change in her. He'd never experienced such openhearted passion, such fearless devotion. She'd given herself to him now, heart and soul, held nothing back. She touched him constantly and was always reaching over for a kiss. She told him that she loved him again and again, and each time he repeated the words back to her Carrie's face would light up with brilliant new joy.

She didn't seem to notice that the more he said *I love you*, the more flat and dull his voice became.

Now, she was upstairs packing Henry's baby clothes for their trip to Seattle. They would get married in her hometown tomorrow, with her family in attendance. When he'd agreed to her plan, she'd thrown her arms around him and wept.

"You are so good to me," she'd whispered. "Thank you

for understanding. You are the most wonderful, kind man in the world."

Wonderful? Kind? Because he was allowing her to have her family at her wedding instead of bullying her into an instant drive-through wedding in Las Vegas?

Théo was starting to feel a constant pain that started at the base of his skull and then radiated down his spine to the vicinity of his heart. Or at least the place where his heart should be.

He had lied to her. He'd lured her into marriage under false pretenses. Théo tried to tell himself that it was for a good cause—to raise his son in a solid home—but he knew his motivation hadn't been entirely noble.

He couldn't bear the thought of any man touching Carrie. He couldn't endure the idea of her ever looking up so breathlessly, with such tender love in her eyes, into the face of another. Her love belonged to Théo—only to him.

Even though he was a selfish liar who did not love her.

Pacing the length of his dark, masculine study as Carrie packed bags upstairs for a flight that would leave in an hour, Théo tried desperately to shrug off his conscience.

He'd won everything he ever wanted. But at what price? Was this another Açoazul S.A.? A Brazilian steel company bought dear, not remotely worth the price he'd paid?

And what would it do to Carrie, to be broken up for her most valuable assets?

Her *assets*. He froze in place, clawing his hair back with one hand. Carrie wasn't a business. She was the kindest, sweetest woman he'd ever known. And her most valuable assets weren't just her skills as a mother, or her passion as a wife. It wasn't even the warmth and comfort she brought to his cold *château*.

It was the light in her eyes. Her cheerful optimism. Her belief in the best in people. Her ideals and dreams were the core of her. If Théo married her, ruthlessly letting that light in her eyes go dim as she realized his deception, he would kill the best part of her.

Her heart.

He wasn't taking her to a wedding, or even a funeral, he realized. He was plotting her murder.

Melodramatic nonsense, he told himself angrily. But it felt true. Had Théo ever once known what it felt like before to be truly loved? Had his home ever felt so warm before her arrival? Had he ever known such depths of passionate ecstasy with any woman?

He didn't want to let her go. Ever.

But if he tricked her into marrying him, everything he admired most about Carrie—her cheerful selflessness, her hopefulness, her dreamy, idealistic heart—would be destroyed.

Grinding his teeth, he stared at all the leatherbound books on the other side of his study. He'd told himself that he had no choice but to be ruthless—for his son's sake. But the truth was that Henry would always be happy with Carrie as his mother. He'd have a wonderful childhood in Seattle, playing baseball with kids in the neighborhood, part of a community, loved by all his cousins and grandparents.

What could Théo offer him except for a large bank account and a drafty gilded *château*?

"The only rich family is one that is filled with love."

He thought about his own lonely upbringing. He'd never felt like he had a home. But even so, even at eight years old, he'd been glad when his parents had separated. Living in the same house with parents who coldly despised each other had been painful. Especially since, even as a child, Théo had known *he* was the shackle that imprisoned his parents together.

He thought of the beauty and hope in Carrie's eyes when she'd spoken of the man she would someday love.

Théo ground his teeth, feeling like he wanted to punch the wall.

It doesn't matter what she wants, he told himself angrily. *I won't give them up. My son is my blood. Carrie will be my wife. I will never let her be loved by another.*

But could he selfishly possess her when he knew it would destroy the light in her that he loved the most?

Clutching his hands into fists, he closed his eyes. He took a deep breath. When he opened his eyes, he stared through the window at the blue sky, at the beauty of the gardens and olive groves stretching toward the craggy mountains.

Then he reached for his phone.

An hour later Carrie knocked on the door to his study, then peeked around the door.

"Is this what happens when you own the plane?" she teased him. "You can keep everyone waiting while you check your email? Even Lilley is already waiting in the car—"

Her voice was cut off when she saw another man in the study. Rising from the desk, from the papers where he'd just affixed his final signature, Théo nodded his lawyer's dismissal.

"I don't like this," the man said grimly in French.

"I don't expect you to," Théo replied in the same language, coldly. The man stalked out of the study, brushing by Carrie. And Théo looked at her, knowing it was the last moment she would love him.

She'd never looked so beautiful. No woman on earth could compare. Her clothes were just jeans and a simple polka-dotted blouse. She wore no makeup but the glow of happiness, and her hair was swept back in a glossy ponytail. Her only jewelry was the engagement ring sparkling on her finger. But the marble-size diamond wasn't half as brilliant as the love and light shining from her hazel eyes.

Théo felt a sharp lump in his throat.

"What was that all about?" Carrie asked, glancing behind her to where the lawyer had disappeared.

He cleared his throat, but it still took several seconds before he could speak over the razor blade in his throat. "That's Jacques Menton. My head attorney."

"Finishing up some business before we leave? That's good." She gave him an arch, impish grin. "Because once we're married you're all mine. The honeymoon will last a year. Maybe two."

This hurt more than he'd thought. He swallowed. "I have to tell you something."

She smiled back at him, happiness and trust shining through her. "What's that, my love?"

His knees felt weak. He sat down heavily in his desk chair. He had to get this over with. Get her out of here as quickly as possible, before his will failed.

He looked up at her. "I've known almost the whole time that Henry is my son."

Her smile widened, her eyes glowing with pure adoration. "You realized I wouldn't lie to you?"

"I got the results of the paternity test almost immediately." He reached for her hand, then suddenly knew that if he touched her he'd never be able to get through this. He placed his hands flat on the desk. "Before I'd even bought that ring for you, I already knew."

Carrie looked down at the sparkling jewel, then back at him, bewildered. "Why didn't you tell me?"

"Isn't it obvious?" he said grimly. "So I'd have time to seduce you into bed and make you agree to my proposal."

The light in her eyes faded. Then a new thought occurred

to her, and she looked up with a beaming smile. "And I had time to teach you how to love—so we're even."

The light and joy in her eyes made his heart stop in his chest.

This was the moment. He had to do it.

"But I don't, Carrie," he said in a low voice.

She tilted her head guilelessly, still happy, only slightly confused. "Don't what?"

Pushing his arms against his desk, he rose to his feet. He looked straight into her eyes, like he was looking at an enemy over the barrel of a rifle. "I don't love you."

Her face went pale. "What?"

"You heard me." He pushed the papers he'd just signed across the desk toward her. "I've just signed a custody agreement. We'll share custody of Henry, but you'll have physical custody. I have created an extremely generous financial arrangement for you both. Neither you nor in fact anyone in your family needs ever work again, if you do not wish."

Carrie looked as if he'd just kicked her in the face. Her creamy rose-pink skin suddenly had the cold green pallor of a corpse.

"You do love me," she choked out. "I know you do. You said—"

"It was a lie." He looked away. "You'll be better off without me, Carrie," he said. "You and Henry will both be better off with your family. You will find a man who can truly love you. A man who will—"

Deserve you, he'd been going to say, but his voice cut off.

She lifted her chin. "You *love* me. I've felt it."

He was going to have to be brutal. "You were right all along," he said roughly. "I only wanted you when I couldn't have you. But now you've become so unbearably clingy..."

She gasped.

"I'm sorry, *ma petite,*" he said coldly, "but I don't want

a wife or a child anymore. I will always love my son, and I tried my best to love you. But I'm not capable of it." Clenching his jaw, he looked straight into her face. "You need to find a man who is."

She didn't answer. She was visibly trembling. Her eyes looked huge in her white face.

"You…don't want us?" she whispered.

It ripped his guts out. But he took the pain and forced himself to keep going, to do what was best for Carrie and his son.

"No," he ground out. "I don't want you."

Hearing him speak those words was like feeling a dagger slicing past her rib cage, straight to her heart.

For the past day and a half she'd been so happy. When he'd told her in Paris that he loved her she'd been shocked, overwhelmed by joy. Every time she'd made him repeat the words that he loved her—every time he'd touched her and shown her his love with more than words—she'd been filled with a happiness so complete she'd thought she might die of it.

And now the end. He didn't love her. He was already tired of her.

"Love always ends," he'd said. *"And it usually ends badly."*

Tearfully, she shook her head. "I can't believe this."

"I will always take care of you both," he said in a low voice. He looked at her and his black eyes glittered, soulless and deep. "Because your happiness is more important to me than anything. More important than my own."

"And yet you're throwing us away?" she choked out. "Just like last year. Because I love you too much? Because I was clingy?"

"Yes," he said coldly, turning away. Pushing the file of papers toward her on the deck, he glared at her. "Take it."

Staring at the file as if it were poison that would kill her with a single touch, she shook her head wordlessly. If she didn't touch the custody papers, if she didn't have physical proof of his words, maybe she could pretend for a few more moments that this wasn't happening—that it was all some kind of nightmare and she'd wake up in his strong, protective arms.

Coming around the desk, Théo forcibly thrust the folder into her hand. She felt it there, and her heart cracked in her chest. Some part of her had always known this would happen, even as she'd tried to believe her dreams might come true.

But she should have known. She should have known a man like Théo St. Raphaël would never love any woman for long…

"Now go back to America and your family," he said brutally. "I'm done with you."

Carrie didn't even remember leaving the study. But suddenly she found herself outside, and the chauffeur was opening the back door. Numbly, she got in the car beside Henry's baby seat.

"Where's Théo?" Lilley asked from the front passenger seat. Then she got a good look at Carrie. "What's wrong?"

Feeling like she was going to be sick, Carrie slowly turned to face her. "The wedding is off," she said faintly. "I'm going home alone. So you don't have to come."

"What?" Lilley's loud voice made the baby start to cry.

"Théo doesn't love me," Carrie whispered. "He wants his freedom."

Lilley stared at her, then shook her head. "No. No way! I've seen the way he looks at you."

"It was a lie." Carrie looked dully out the window. The *château* looked empty and cold. Even Provence itself seemed to have lost its vibrancy and color. "The wedding is off," she said again.

"Did he say why?"

"He said I was clingy."

Fury etched every line of Lilley's plump, sweet face. "If that's how he's going to treat you, then—then…I quit!"

Carrie looked at her in shock. "But Théo's your cousin!"

"*Distant* cousin. And not nearly distant enough at this moment," Lilley grumbled. Getting out of the car, she moved to sit in the back near Carrie. As she reached across the baby seat to pat her gently on the shoulder, Lilley leaned forward to the driver. "Well, what are you waiting for? The airport!"

Tears of relief filled Carrie's eyes. She wouldn't have to face the long flight alone. "Thank you," she whispered. "But what will you do in Seattle?"

As the car hummed along the road leading from Gavaudan Castle, Lilley Smith settled back in the leather seat and her eyes brightened. "I'll go see my boyfriend in San Francisco."

"You have a boyfriend?" Carrie said in surprise.

Lilley's face fell. "Sort of," she mumbled.

"I hope you'll be happy," Carrie said.

Lilley snorted. "Huh. Don't worry about me. And Théo will soon regret what he's done. Believe me, he…"

But Carrie couldn't listen as she prattled on. Leaning her head against the cool glass of the window, she stared out at the streaks of red flowers and green vineyards streaking by in a blur. She felt limp, like her very blood was burning inside her body, pulsing from the radioactive glowing core of anguish that had once been her heart.

Closing her eyes, she had a sudden sharp memory of his haunted face. *"You'll be better off without me, Carrie... You will find a man who can truly love you."*

The car pulled to a stop. She opened her eyes to see the tarmac of the nearby private airport. Lilley got out first, snapping out the car seat to carry Henry in the cushioned baby carrier. Carrie climbed out behind her, nearly stumbling as she made her way across the smooth, dry tarmac toward the steps leading to Théo's jet.

With a shuddering breath, she looked behind her at the beautiful land of vivid beauty and deep love she knew she'd never see again.

A week ago she would have been thrilled to leave here. She now had everything she'd once wanted. Théo would be a part-time father to their son, but Carrie would not be forced to a life of heartbreak as his wife. She didn't need to look for a waitressing job. She could spend her time raising her son, just as she most wanted. Théo had fulfilled her childhood dream.

The thought made her stop in her tracks. He'd had her in his grasp. She'd been ready to marry him. *Why* had he shown mercy? *Why* had he let her go?

One moment he'd been determined to marry her. He'd moved heaven and earth to seduce her. His desire for her had only grown as the week had passed. Then, at the moment of victory, he'd suddenly let her go.

Carrie closed her eyes, recalling his face in the shadowy light of his study. She'd been so overwhelmed by her own grief and pain that she hadn't noticed the tight expression of his eyes, the hard set of his jaw, the odd pallor of his skin.

"I will always take care of you both," he'd said. *"Your happiness is more important to me than anything. More important than my own."*

She slowly opened her eyes.

Théo hadn't wanted to let her go. He'd sacrificed his own wants for hers.

Why?

With a ragged intake of breath, she stared out at the magical landscape around her. Provence was full of color again—color so vibrant and rough and bright it hurt her eyes.

Théo *did* love her. He'd proved that with his actions. He loved her more than she'd ever even imagined.

"Carrie?" Lilley called, peeking around the doorway of the jet with the baby in her arms. "Everything all right?"

In the far distance Carrie thought she saw the Mediterranean. The sun was just starting to lower in the sky like a ball of golden fire against the sapphire sea.

"Yes," she whispered. She exhaled, and as she looked up a slow-rising smile lit up her face brighter than Christmas morning. "Everything is going to be all right."

From his study, Théo had watched the black sedan disappear down the avenue of trees from his *château*. He'd stood by the window until he couldn't even see the cloud of dust.

Carrie and Henry would be happy in Seattle. He knew it. But he…

Théo looked around at his study. The castle felt empty as a tomb. No laughter. No warmth. No baby. No family.

No Carrie.

Wearily, Théo sat back in his chair and rubbed his forehead with his hands. He felt a strange pressure in his chest, right above his solar plexus—a tightening of his heart that was about as tiny and suggestive as cardiac arrest.

He felt…

Nothing, he told himself fiercely. He felt absolutely nothing. He'd left women before. He'd even left *Carrie* before.

But he hadn't felt remotely like this. When he'd left Carrie last year he'd been angry and regretful, like a child forced to surrender a favorite toy.

This was different. What had changed?

Théo folded his arms, staring out the window. Carrie meant more to him now than just incredible sex, more than soul-searing passion. He knew her. He cared for her. Admired her. Respected her. And more...

Infatuation, he told himself furiously. Illusion. He could have another beautiful woman at the castle within the hour. He could replace Carrie easily.

But his soul felt the lie.

He took a shuddering breath, his hands tightening into fists as he stared out at the distant horizon toward the airport he couldn't see beyond the southern hills.

He knew he could never replace Carrie. The mother of his child. The woman he'd gotten to know outside of bed. Kindhearted, idealistic, romantic, passionate. No woman alive could compare to her. Her innocent faith had made him into a better man. Made him want to be the man she'd thought he was.

She'd brought him to life. And he'd let her go.

For her own good, he told himself fiercely. She deserved a man who could love her. A man who would put her needs above his own. A man who would always seek to protect her.

Even from himself.

For several seconds blood roared in his ears as he stared blindly through the window. He was willing to suffer anything, endure any pain, in order to secure Carrie's happiness. Did that mean he loved her?

He felt like all joy had died, vanished from the earth in a puff of smoke, from the instant she'd left. Did that mean he loved her?

He felt like he'd give up his billion-dollar business, lose his fortune, his status, his homes—if he could only have Carrie and his son at his side.

She'd seen him at his worst, but still found it in herself to forgive, to love him. He couldn't quite understand the miracle of her heart.

For him, loving her was easy.

His eyes widened.

He loved her.

He was completely, totally, insanely in love with her. It wasn't illusion. It wasn't fantasy. It was the most real thing in existence. The only thing that would live after death. *He loved her.*

His heart expanded in his chest, then suddenly constricted. He sucked in his breath, then narrowed his eyes.

He had to catch that plane.

Flinging back the door of the study, Théo raced down the hallway, his footsteps pounding heavily against the marble floor. Grabbing a key in his garage, he jumped into his fastest car and roared down the road so fast he almost flew.

He arrived at the private airport, sliding to a stop with a scatter of gravel. He ran through the cavernous, empty hangar out onto the tarmac.

But he was too late.

He watched his plane take off and soar into the sky.

"No," he whispered, his breath coming hard. He covered his face with his hands. *"No."*

"Théo?"

He whirled around. Carrie stood quietly by the wide open door of the hangar, holding their baby in her arms.

"You ran right by me," she said awkwardly. "You went so fast I couldn't—"

Théo didn't wait. He didn't think. He just went straight to her and took her in his arms.

Entwining his hands in her hair, he kissed her with all the passion and love he'd kept hidden in his heart for thirty-six years. Waiting for her. Only for her.

As he felt her kiss him back the frozen wall inside him finally broke, allowing life and sun inside his soul. He pulled away, stroking her cheeks as he looked down into her eyes.

"I love you, Carrie," he whispered. "I love you."

* * *

His kiss was gentle, deep and true. It was a promise.

When he finally pulled away, his voice was low and rough as he spoke words of love like a prayer.

She looked up at him, blinking through the tears of joy that filled her eyes. "I knew it."

"You knew?"

"I—hoped."

Passionately, Théo kissed her again, and it took several minutes and a baby's protest about being squashed before they remembered to come up for air.

He leaned his forehead against hers, holding the baby tenderly between them. "Thank you," he said in a low voice. "Thank you for believing in me." He looked back at the sky. The plane was long gone—nothing more than a black speck in the sky. "But who is on my plane?"

She shook her head with a laugh as tears streamed unchecked down her face. "Lilley. She's quit her job, by the way, and gone to see her boyfriend in San Francisco."

"She has a boyfriend?"

Carrie struggled to remember what Lilley had said. "A sort-of one, I think."

"He can't possibly deserve her." Théo looked at her with an intake of breath. "Just as I don't deserve you. But I'm asking for you to give me one more chance." His dark eyes searched hers. "Let me try to be the man of your dreams. I swear to you I will love and cherish and protect you for the rest of your life—"

She pressed a finger to his lips, stopping him. For an instant his handsome, hard-edged face fell into an expression of despair.

"You already are the man of my dreams. I've always known that." She looked up at him. "Even when I hated you I dreamed of you."

He cupped her cheek. His face shone with adoration.

"You don't just see the best in people, Carrie," he said quietly, looking deeply into her eyes. "You see the truth of what they most wish they could be."

Wrapping his arms around her, he kissed her with intensity and fire, causing her to utterly melt against him. It was, she thought afterward, dazed, the best kiss of her whole life.

Or so she thought until two days later, when he kissed her at their wedding in a beachside park in West Seattle. Her friends and family applauded wildly after the simple outdoor ceremony, with the backdrop of Seattle's skyscrapers across the bay. A moment before it had been merely misty, but the second they spoke their vows the lowering clouds broke at last, pouring showers of rain.

As Carrie looked at her new husband, both of them utterly soaked, she helplessly tried to use her small bouquet of sunflowers as an umbrella over their heads. They both laughed.

Smiling, Théo lowered his head to kiss her, whispering, "*Je t'adore,* Madame la Comtesse."

She threw her arms around his neck and kissed him with all her heart. And then they gathered their baby son—in his little suit, with his ring-bearer's pillow—in their arms, to kiss his chubby cheeks and protect him from the rain.

As she watched her new husband shake the hands of her soaked, smiling family and friends, Carrie had never been so happy.

Life was full of color, she realized. Even on the grayest day, love was all around her—like rainbows in a storm. And now she was Théo's wife, Carrie knew her life would always be full of vibrant reds and yellows and violets and bright blue skies. No matter what rains might come.

* * * * *

THE SANDOVAL BABY
Kate Hewitt

CHAPTER ONE

RAFE SANDOVAL pulled his car to the kerb and stared at the seemingly innocuous terraced house he'd parked in front of. It was a bit shabby, on an ordinary little street, in a bland, faceless suburb of London. And his son—his *son*—was inside.

Rafe's fingers curled around the steering wheel until his bones ached. He felt a tidal rush of emotions pour through him before he pushed it all down, forced himself to maintain an icy calm. He needed it now, when he was so close. Close to his son.

He took a deep breath, let it out slowly, and then turned off the ignition and slid from the car. The slam of the door echoed in the street and he surveyed the little house with its blank windows and unkempt garden. A single geranium in a cracked pot stood on the step, looking woefully bedraggled. A blue rubber ball had been left in the garden, lost in the weeds. Rafe curled his lip at the pathetic sight, yet he could not quite keep some small part of him from being touched by these signs of life. The life his son had lived for three years without any knowledge or awareness of his father.

Or Rafe's awareness of his son.

He reached for the tarnished brass knocker and let it fall sharply three times. Then he waited, the tension coiling inside him, demanding release. After years of longing for a child, years of being lied to, he was finally so close. Only one woman stood in his way.

The door opened and Rafe gazed dispassionately at the figure standing there. She looked remarkably composed, without even a flicker of surprise at seeing the stranger on her doorstep. Of course his solicitor had informed her of the arrangements.

'Señor Sandoval, hello. I've been expecting you. Won't you come in?' She stepped aside, and Rafe entered the cramped foyer, taking in the faded wallpaper, the worn carpet, the clutter of boots by the foot of the stairs. He could hardly believe his son—his heir—had been living like this.

'You must be Miss Clark?' he said, turning to face her. She had surprisingly striking features. Her pale face was heart-shaped, her eyes a cool grey, revealing nothing. Her hair, pulled back into a neat ponytail, was a deep red, almost magenta, yet he didn't think she dyed it. Her eyebrows, arching over those clear, expressionless eyes, were the same colour. 'Yes. Please call me Freya.'

Rafe inclined his head in acknowledgement, but did not reply. He had no intention of staying long enough to call her anything. He wanted his son. That was all.

Freya gestured to the little parlour off the hall. 'Won't you come in? Max is sleeping for the moment, but he should wake up soon.'

Max. Maximo. The name was both familiar and foreign. He wondered why Rosalia had chosen the name—*if* she'd chosen the name. How involved had she been in the life of their son? How much had this woman been involved, and how much did she know? He had so many questions, yet he did not intend to find answers from this stranger.

He did not want to sit and make pleasantries over a tepid cup of tea. Still, Rafe acknowledged, forcing his impatience and his anger back, this woman had cared for his son for most of his young life. Talking to her was necessary, perhaps invaluable. Undoubtedly there were things he needed to know. Nodding again, he followed her into the parlour, which was as shabby as the rest of the dismal little house.

'I realise this is a strange situation,' Freya said. She perched on the edge of a straight-backed chair, her legs crossed at the ankles. She looked, Rafe thought, as if she were interviewing for a position at finishing school.

He remained standing by the door. 'Yes, it is strange,' he agreed tersely, 'although I do not blame you for that.'

Freya Clark raised her eyebrows. 'Indeed, Señor Sandoval,' she said coolly. 'I did not know of your whereabouts until the solicitor informed me a few days ago and requested that I bring Max for a paternity test.'

She spoke with a hint of censure, but Rafe had no intention of explaining anything to her—certainly not how he'd craved reassurance that Max was truly his, how much reason he'd had to expect he was not.

'I realise it all happened very quickly,' he said coolly. Less than a week ago he'd been informed his ex-wife had died in a car crash. Then another, even more shocking call: he had a son.

A son he'd never known about. A son his wife had never told him about, even though she must have known she was pregnant when she'd left him. Even though he'd been paying her maintenance for the four years since their divorce. Glancing around the parlour, with its secondhand suite and faded curtains, Rafe knew where his money *hadn't* been going.

'And I did not know of my son's whereabouts,' he countered, 'or even his existence.' Not until his solicitor had rung him. Not until he'd had the results of the paternity test, confirming that Max really was his.

Something flickered in Freya Clark's silver-grey eyes,

like a ripple in water. Was it guilt? Had she participated in Rosalia's deception? She looked as if she was hiding something with her carefully closed expression, those blank eyes, and Rafe had no intention of trusting her.

Still, it hardly mattered. He was taking Max back to Spain and he would hire a reliable governess there. He had no need of this woman, with her strange silver eyes and her remote composure. He did not want any vestige of his son's—or his wife's—former life cluttering up their future as a family.

'I'm very glad the solicitor was able to locate you,' Freya said, and again Rafe felt that flicker of suspicion. She did not sound very sincere—or was he simply being cynical? God knew he had enough reason to be cynical where women were concerned. Not one had deserved his trust or love.

He pushed the question aside, too impatient to deal with it, or the woman who had caused it. The sooner he—and Max—were gone from this awful place the better.

'Yes, indeed,' he agreed pleasantly, although he knew she heard the thread of steel in his voice. He'd had enough of pleasantries. 'When Max wakes up you can pack his things. I intend to return to Spain tonight.'

Any faint hope that Rafe Sandoval might not be interested in his son crumbled to dust in light of his coldly delivered statement. And, Freya told herself fiercely, that was fine. That was good. Max needed to be with his father—the only family he had now. During the last week she'd told herself that again and again. Yet still the idea of losing him so quickly, so coldly, of him being ripped away from her just as—

Freya stopped that train of thought immediately and made herself smile at Rafe. 'I can certainly understand your haste, Señor Sandoval—'

'Can you, Miss Clark?'

His dark eyes flashed dangerously, and she knew he was mocking her. He was a beautiful man, with his high cheekbones and the dark slashes of his eyebrows a bold contrast to the sensual fullness of his lips. Although his hair was cut quite short, it looked silky and soft, and he couldn't quite keep it from flopping over his forehead. She imagined that annoyed him. He'd raked his long, brown fingers through his unruly fringe three times since he'd come into the house. A tiny insecurity, but it made him seem more human. More approachable.

And this was the man Rosalia had never wanted to speak of. A man she'd had to escape because he was so hard and cold and even cruel. Freya knew better than to believe every accusation Rosalia had hissed out in her anger and fear, but Rafe Sandoval did have an intimidating presence. She could sense a leashed anger emanating from this powerful man; it vibrated in every taut line of his muscular body. His fingers clenched into a fist at his sides and then straightened out again. Twice.

'I can,' she replied steadily. 'I know you must be eager to spend time with your son, and get to know him—' Actually, she didn't know that. From everything Rosalia had said, Rafe wasn't interested in Max. Never had been. Then the solicitor had rung and told her Max's father had been located, had never known about his son, and was coming to collect him as soon as possible. Freya's safe little world had suddenly been rent apart—the truth she'd built it on that Max had no one but her now shown for a lie.

Yet she should have known it would happen at some point. She was Max's nanny, not his mother. She was temporary, expendable, replaceable. She'd always known that, even if she'd managed to pretend otherwise while Rosalia had partied in London and she and Max had lived their separate, contented existence here. Even if she'd let herself love him, had been as good as a mother to him for over three years. She'd still known, and it was that knowledge that was breaking her heart now.

'Indeed.' Rafe's tone was forbidding, the word clearly a close to the conversation. His dark gaze flicked towards the stairs.

Freya felt a rush of gratitude that Max had been so tired from his morning at playgroup that he'd fallen asleep. A small mercy, but a crucial one. She needed this time to convince Rafe Sandoval to take her to Spain with him.

And, from the ill-disguised impatience on his coldly handsome face, it wasn't going to be an easy job.

'Did the solicitor say anything to you about Max?' she asked.

Rafe's fingers clenched once more. 'He told me that he was my son, and the paternity test verified that. Is there more I need to know?' From the sardonic note in his voice Freya knew he was being sarcastic, and she felt a lick of anger, which she suppressed. Losing her temper would not help her in this situation.

'Actually, there is. Max has just lost his mother—'

'I'm well aware.'

'And is in a fragile state,' Freya continued, ignoring him. 'He needs consistency, stability.' *He needs me.* She barely kept from saying the words. 'Rushing him off to a foreign country is not the best thing for him now.'

'Being without his father for three years wasn't the best thing either,' Rafe returned, an edge to his voice.

'True, but there is no point adding one hardship on top of another.'

Rafe stared at her, his gaze icily assessing. 'What do you suggest, Miss Clark?' he finally asked, his tone as cold as his look.

Freya took a deep breath. 'I have been the one consistent

element in Max's life,' she began evenly. *I love him.* She swallowed down the words, knowing they wouldn't help. They might even hurt. They certainly wouldn't sway a man like Rafe—a man who, according to his ex-wife, had no interest in love at all. A man who was staring at her with cold impatience. 'I think I should stay with Max as he makes the transition—'

'I intend finding a suitable carer in Spain,' Rafe returned flatly.

'There's no need,' Freya argued, her voice calm. She felt as if her heart were flinging itself against her chest, but she'd never let Rafe Sandoval see how much this meant to her—how much she'd come to love Max over the last three years. He was the only person she'd let into her heart in ten years. Since—

No. She would not think about that. She lifted her chin. 'You have a suitable carer right here.'

Rafe let out a slow breath, studying her. Freya waited, knowing judgement could come swiftly, in seconds. 'I would prefer,' he said finally, 'to have a completely fresh start.'

'Understandable,' Freya countered, knowing how acrimonious the Sandovals' divorce must have been. 'But fresh starts are not always good for children. Max was happy here.'

Rafe glanced around the little parlour, which Freya knew was a bit...worn. 'Really?'

Scepticism dripped from his voice, and Freya stiffened. 'You don't need a mansion or a flashy car to make a child happy.'

'How about a father?'

'Yes, exactly. Someone to—' Once again she swallowed down that dangerous L-word.

Rafe narrowed his eyes. 'I will give you severance pay,'

he said, his look and tone both assessing. Suspicious. 'A generous package. So if it's money you're concerned about—'

'It's not money,' Freya replied sharply. Colour flashed into her face. 'It's Max.'

Rafe arched an eyebrow. 'You care for him?'

'Of course I do.'

'Enough to travel to a foreign country?'

'I'm familiar with Spain,' Freya admitted, trying not to show how reluctant she was to reveal that fact. She didn't want to think about the last time she'd been to Spain, or the mistakes she'd made. The loss she'd endured. She *never* thought about that. She met Rafe's speculative gaze clearly, refusing to allow even the faintest flicker of emotion to cross her face.

'I'd prefer,' he said, 'to have someone care for Max who speaks Spanish.'

Freya could not keep the triumph from her voice as she told him, 'I'm fluent in Spanish.'

Rafe smiled faintly as he conceded the point in their power struggle. 'You are full of surprises, Miss Clark.'

'I don't mean to be. But Ro— Max's mother wanted me to speak both Spanish and English to Max.'

'I'm glad,' Rafe said, in a voice that was carefully, painfully bland, 'that she did not keep Max from his Spanish heritage.' His mouth hardened into a thin line. 'Only his Spanish father.'

Freya said nothing. She'd had no great affection for Rosalia Sandoval, but she'd felt sorry for her. The woman had been clearly unhappy, and underneath the anger Freya had thought she'd seen hurt. At one point, Freya suspected, Rosalia had been deeply in love with her husband.

Rafe straightened, glancing around the little parlour with an expression of dismissal. Freya felt her heart lodge like a stone inside her. 'I appreciate all you've done for Max,' he said briskly, 'but children adapt. And Max is going to have a completely new life—one in which he will not want for anything.' His expression softened for only a second, those dark eyes shadowed with something like pity. 'On occasion a fresh start is exactly what is needed.'

His tone was so unbearably final that Freya could not keep herself from retorting sharply, 'I doubt Social Services will agree.'

Rafe tensed with a predatory stillness, all traces of pity vanished. 'I hope,' he said in a dangerously soft voice, 'you have not involved Social Services in the life of my son.'

Freya bit her lip. She'd just made a critical error—one that might cost her any possibility of staying with Max. Although, she acknowledged with a stab of pain, that possibility already seemed depressingly remote.

Rafe was still levelling her with a hard stare, compelling Freya to confession. 'No,' she admitted, 'I haven't.' Rafe's solicitor had been clear on that point.

This last week, the week after Rosalia's death, had been a terrible blur. Hearing of Rosalia's accident, arranging the funeral, seeing the solicitor, and all the while trying to comfort and reassure Max, whose world had collapsed without him even realising it. And then the sudden, startling news that Rafe Sandoval, the man Rosalia had seemed to hate, was coming to England to take custody of his son.

All Freya was meant to do, the solicitor had told her with unctuous urbanity, was bring Max for a blood test to confirm paternity, and then wait until he arrived. Rafe had been unreachable when Rosalia had died, which was why he'd missed the funeral. The solicitor had said something smarmy about a *very* important business deal in South America.

Freya had constructed a picture of Rafe Sandoval in her mind of a man too caught up with his own affairs to care about his ex-wife—or his son. A man who insisted on genetic testing before he so much as stirred himself to consider the child that had been left in his care. A man who would be more than willing to hand over such care to the nanny already in place.

And now, in the cold, hard light of reality—of *Rafe*—she knew it wasn't going to happen like that at all.

Yet during the last endless week she'd come to the impossible, emotional realisation that she could not hand Max over to a stranger. For a while she'd been able to look at it with her usual remote composure, but now, when it came to packing his things, saying goodbye…

She couldn't. She wouldn't. She'd spent the last three years loving Max, and she wasn't ready to give that up. She'd given up once before, and she couldn't do it again. Doing it again would destroy her.

And so she'd convinced herself that Rafe Sandoval would not want such a thing for his son. He would surely see the sense and have the sensitivity of allowing his son to remain with the one person he'd bonded with.

Apparently not.

But then this was not a man known for his sensitivity. Internet searches had told Freya all she needed to know about Rafe Sandoval's business practices: he waited until a company was struggling, desperate and in its death throes, and then he moved in and bought it, dismantling it for its valuable parts with ruthless efficiency. They even called him El Tiburón—the shark—and she could see how the name fitted. Could imagine him cruising hungrily through the business world, looking for his next prey to devour.

He was approaching his son with the same kind of cold-blooded logic. Here was a company to manage; she was an unnecessary part. How could she convince him otherwise?

'Freya…' Max's sweetly childish voice drifted from upstairs.

Freya and Rafe both froze, staring at each other.

Max called again, more insistently. 'Fre—ya!'

A muscle flickered in Rafe's jaw and his fingers clenched again. Freya swallowed, her heart starting its fearful, frantic beat once more. Then simultaneously they both moved towards the stairs.

CHAPTER TWO

ALTHOUGH he wanted to take the stairs two at a time, Rafe held back. He had enough sense to know that barging into his sleepy son's room was hardly the best introduction. He didn't want to frighten the child.

He followed Freya down the narrow hallway to the back bedroom. Although all he wanted was to see his son, his gaze was momentarily diverted by the sight of Freya leaning over the bed. Her clothes were boring—a cheap black skirt and a white button-down shirt—but there was something so gracefully maternal about her movements as she sat on the edge of the bed, a smile softening those cool features. She looked as lovely and remote as a painting—distant, decorous, and yet also, he realised, desirable.

She brushed the silky hair away from his son's forehead, and Rafe turned to look upon the child he'd never known he had.

The child he'd always wanted.

Max.

The little boy scrubbed his eyes with his fists, then blinked sleepily, smiling up at Freya. 'I had a funny dream...' He paused, the smile freezing on his face as he stared past Freya to Rafe. Max shrank into Freya's side, his eyes rounding with uncertainty and perhaps even fear.

Rafe stood there, his throat working as he tried to think

of the right words to say. He'd never been speechless before, yet now his mind was empty. The realisation of his own child was thudding through him, obliterating thought.

'Max, this is a friend,' Freya said, shifting over on the bed so Rafe could see his son.

Max buried his head in Freya's lap and Rafe watched as she continued to stroke his hair with pale, slender fingers.

Her words caught up with him and his frozen brain finally thawed for thought. A *friend*? Freya glanced at him sharply, and he saw a warning in her eyes. Anger spiked through Rafe. He was not a friend. He would not begin this most precious relationship with a lie. Yet, even as he opened his mouth to deny her claim, he realised how difficult it would be to explain the truth to his son. The anger hardened inside him. Already Freya Clark had put him in an impossible position. Already she had tricked him, showing him that he was right not to trust her. Trust anyone.

He clenched his fists, then forced them flat again. He wanted to tell Max to get up, that they were going; he wanted to hug him. He knew both would terrify the child, so he clung to his last shred of patience and took his cue from Miss Clark.

'Hello, Max,' he said, and his son buried his face against Freya's shoulder. 'Yes, I am a friend. And I'm so very happy to meet you.'

Freya heard the raw note of emotion in Rafe's voice, and it surprised her. Moved her, even. For, after everything Rosalia had said—'He never loved me. He doesn't know how to love.'—she hadn't really expected Rafe to feel anything for his son. He was cold, cynical, unable to love. That was what Rosalia had told her, what the tabloids and gossip magazines said. El Tiburón.

And she'd been counting on that, counting on the fact that

Rafe was too busy with his professional life to deal with his son properly; she'd thought—hoped—he'd be glad for Freya to do it, despite her connection with Rosalia.

Yet hearing the rawness of Rafe's voice, seeing how he looked almost hungrily at his child, made Freya realise uncomfortably, painfully, that nothing about this situation was what she'd thought. That maybe Rafe wasn't what she'd thought.

Max peeked at Rafe from behind her shoulder, curious now, but still shy, and Freya stood up from the bed. 'Why don't we go downstairs and have a snack?'

Max slipped his little hand in hers, and Freya led him downstairs, Rafe following behind. She could feel the tension and even the anger emanating from the man; it rolled off him in waves. She felt her own body tense in response, her heart thudding despite her determination to remain calm. To feel calm.

Already this man was making her feel too much. She'd been carefully, comfortably numb for so long, and it was strange and unsettling how he'd managed to strip that away from her within minutes. Her mind and body's basic response to him was alarming. Frightening, even.

Unless, of course, it wasn't him. It was simply the situation. The possibility of losing Max, and even of travelling to Spain, had brought too many painful memories to the fore. Memories she'd spent the last ten years trying to forget. And, even though they hurt, it was better than thinking Rafe affected her.

Better than making the mistake—again—of falling for a man's handsome face and then being crushed under his heel. No, she'd learned that lesson all too terribly well. She would not be affected by Rafe Sandoval at all.

Yet she could still feel his presence, even his heat, behind her as she went down the stairs.

The next quarter of an hour was spent dealing with Max, yet Freya knew she could put off another conversation with Rafe for only so long. He loomed like a shadow in the kitchen, watching as she prepared Max a cup of milk and some slices of apple, helping him into his chair while he watched the stranger with wide, solemn eyes.

'Are you a friend of Mummy's?' he finally asked, and the very air seemed to freeze.

Freya was amazed Max had even thought to make such a connection; Rosalia's visits had been infrequent enough to make him stop asking for her. Yet her death, of course, had brought his mother and her absence to the front of his mind, and Freya supposed it was natural for him to attempt to make sense of the recent disorder of his world.

'I knew your mother,' Rafe replied carefully, his voice controlled.

'Were you friends?'

Another agonising pause. Freya watched emotions flicker across Rafe's face: anger foremost, and then uncertainty, perhaps even sorrow. 'Yes,' he finally said, although to Freya the word sounded reluctant. 'We were.'

Max nodded, apparently—and thankfully—satisfied, and while he sipped his milk Freya returned to the kitchen, mindlessly tidying up while she registered Rafe Sandoval's presence near her, felt the force of it like a charismatic and inexorable tug on her body.

'We leave tonight.'

She turned, her heart caught in her chest. 'We?'

Rafe inclined his head. 'I take your point, Miss Clark. Max needs the stability of a familiar care-giver until he settles into his new home.'

Until. The word was ominous. 'Thank you,' she said, her voice cool with dignity. 'I'll pack our bags.'

Rafe nodded, satisfied with her acquiescence. Freya knew

better than to push for more time in England. She'd got what she wanted, and she intended to keep it by asking for no more. Still, the thought of returning to Spain sent a shiver of trepidation and even cold, raw fear through her. She suppressed it, determined to deal only in practicalities.

'I don't think Max has a passport—'

'I can deal with that.' Rafe slipped a mobile phone from his jacket pocket, already punching in numbers. 'I have to make a few preparations for the trip. Be ready by five o'clock.'

Startled, Freya glanced at the clock on the cooker. That was in just over two hours. 'So quick—'

'Yes.' Rafe looked up, and his dark gaze—his eyes were so *black*—pinned Freya in place. 'I conceded to you in this one thing, Miss Clark. Don't look for other concessions.'

Freya swallowed. This felt like a war, yet she could hardly blame Rafe Sandoval for feeling antagonistic. She had seen him as the opposition from the moment she'd heard his name in the solicitor's office.

He's the man who will take Max away from me.

'Just making an observation,' she stated coolly. 'We'll be ready.'

'Good.' Rafe snapped his mobile shut and returned to Max, who had finished his milk and apple slices and was now looking at the two adults in the room with wary expectation. 'Max, how would you like to go on a trip?' Rafe crouched down to Max's eye-level, smiling and assured, while Freya watched on.

'A trip?' Max repeated, and glanced at Freya. She nodded her reassurance.

'Yes, a little holiday, Max. Would you like that?'

'Where are we going?'

'To Spain.' Rafe stood up. 'I have a house there, right in

the mountains. There's a swimming pool too. Do you like to swim?'

Max smiled shyly. 'Yes, I think so.'

'He hasn't been very much,' Freya explained.

Rafe's gaze flicked over her, and when he looked away it felt like a dismissal. 'I'm sure there are many things Max hasn't done,' he said. 'This will be a new experience for him.'

The hint of challenge in his voice made Freya realise how easily Rafe Sandoval was able to put her in her place. He had all the power, all the control.

She only had Max…and for how long?

'We'll both look forward to it,' she said, and with the faintest flicker of a smile Rafe turned away from her to face his son once more.

'I shall see you later, Max. We'll take an aeroplane to Spain. You can even watch a film during the flight.' Max didn't reply, clearly unable to process all these changes in so short a space of time. Rafe gazed at his son, his eyes seeming to turn even blacker, and then slowly—hesitantly—he reached out one hand and very gently, as if Max were made of glass, tousled his hair.

Max flinched a little under the hesitant caress, and to her surprise Freya felt a pang of sympathy and perhaps something else, something deeper and more dangerous, for Rafe.

'He's a bit shy with strangers—aren't you, Max?'

Rafe turned to her, his expression coolly challenging, his voice low enough so only Freya would hear. 'Well, we shan't be strangers for long, shall we?' he said, and with one last smile for his son he left.

Rafe sat in the driver's seat, knowing he needed to put the key in the ignition and drive away. He didn't. Couldn't. His hands were trembling too much.

He let out a slow, shuddery breath, adrenalin, anticipation, and anger racing through him in equal measures. He'd just seen his son. The child he'd always wanted and never thought to have.

The child his ex-wife had tricked him out of...twice.

Rafe forced himself to relax, forced the dark memories back—memories of his own loveless childhood, and then the unhappy years of his marriage. The cold, cold gaze of his father as he surveyed the son he'd never loved. The way he'd often looked past him, as if Rafe wasn't there. As if he didn't want him to be. And only when he was an adult had he learned why.

Things would be different now, Rafe promised himself. A new generation, a new day. He was the father now, not the unwanted child, and he loved his son. Nothing and no one would keep him from Max...and certainly not Freya Clark.

CHAPTER THREE

FREYA settled Max into his seat on Rafe Sandoval's private jet, trying not to show her awe and intimidation at such luxurious surroundings. The scope of Rafe's wealth and power had never been more apparent than now.

Max wriggled, trying to peer out of the window in his excitement, and frustration, exacerbated by her nerves, caused Freya to raise her voice in a way she hardly ever did.

'Max, settle down!'

'He's just excited—aren't you, Max?'

Rafe had appeared behind her without sound or warning, so Freya nearly jumped in surprise. Annoyance bit at her; the last thing she wanted was Rafe Sandoval seeing her lose her temper with his son. She turned around to face Rafe, smiling coolly, composure firmly restored.

'Of course he is. This is an amazing aeroplane.' She looked away from Rafe's dark, knowing gaze to examine the inside of the jet, taking in its leather sofas and teak coffee tables. It looked like an upscale hotel lounge, not a mode of transport.

'We'll be taking off in a few minutes,' Rafe said. 'Once the plane is at altitude, we can have something to eat. I suppose Max must have missed his dinner?'

Freya nodded. She'd spent the two hours between Rafe arriving this afternoon and now sorting and packing their things, answering Max's ceaseless questions, and trying to quell her own nerves. This was so soon, so sudden, so *much*.

She wanted to stay with Max, of course she did. Since hearing about Rafe Sandoval's custody claim a week ago she'd thought of little else. But she hadn't considered how quickly he would move, how much he would want Max... and what it would feel like to return to Spain after all these years.

She pushed that thought—that memory—away. She never thought of her year in Spain, or the endless well of sorrow it opened up inside her. She wouldn't start thinking about it now; she couldn't afford to.

Max was happily looking out of the window now, so Freya took the opportunity to speak privately—and profession-ally—to Rafe. 'I just left the house—locked, of course.'

'My solicitor will deal with it,' Rafe dismissed, the matter dealt with easily, thoughtlessly.

Freya thought of the terraced house where she'd spent so many happy days with Max over the last three years. She'd probably never see it again. Neither would Max. Those days, Rafe was effectively telling her with his dismissal and his dark stare, were over.

She swallowed, the hugeness of Rafe's decision—and her determination to stay with Max—reverberating through her. 'You should sit down,' Rafe told her. 'The plane is about to take off.'

Freya took her seat, holding her hands tightly in her lap, trying to remain calm. The events of the day were catching up with her with dizzying speed. She took a few slow, deep breaths and let them out, hoping Rafe wouldn't notice her little exercise in self-control. She needed it now—needed to steady herself. Feelings and memories lingered on the fringes of her mind, in the recesses of her heart. If she let them, Freya knew, they would take her over completely.

They didn't speak as the plane took to the air, and for the next little while Freya kept herself occupied with Max, pointing things out on the ground, chatting mindlessly about the aeroplane and all its features. She could sense Rafe's presence near her, felt awareness prickle along her skin and coil inside, yet she did not face him. He'd taken out a sheaf of papers, and out of the corner of her eye she saw he was focused on his work—which was just as well. Even just sitting there he was far too distracting. Too tempting.

No, she couldn't think that way. Freya stiffened, appalled by the nature of her own thoughts. She'd kept men strictly off-limits for years, and now this cold-blooded corporate type was causing her to stumble. Surely she was tougher than that? More experienced than that?

Yet, even so, her gaze wandered past Max, now busily exploring the plane, to Rafe. He was tapping a pen against his thigh—the fabric pulled taut over lean, hard muscle—as he gazed, frowning, at the papers spread across the table. Freya couldn't look away, even when he looked up. His gaze settled on his son, and there was such longing and sadness in that dark look that Freya's breath caught in her chest. She was not mistaking the depth of emotion in Rafe's eyes, for she still saw it when his gaze swung to her and pinned her in place. She could not look away...and neither could he. They stared at each other, and Freya felt heat break out over her body. Awareness. *Desire.*

Rafe's gaze moved slowly over her body, and Freya felt her face flush. Then his expression hardened, his mouth thinning, and he looked away. Freya sagged against her seat, amazed and unnerved by how affected she'd been by a simple look. Except there had been nothing simple about it. It had been dark and dangerous and far too tempting.

After dinner—which was thankfully dominated by Max's childish questions—Freya tucked him in and sat stroking his hair until he dropped off to sleep. The flight would land in just another couple of hours, and there was nothing keeping her from talking to Rafe. Why did the thought bother her so much? Why did *he* bother her so much? There was something about him, Freya thought. The blackness of his eyes and the tense energy he radiated, the overwhelming, charismatic *maleness* of him. It made her nervous.

Made her remember.

Which was ridiculous because, while Spain certainly held many painful memories, Rafe Sandoval looked nothing like Timeo. Timeo had been slighter, shorter, less imposing—if charming in his own way. Just thinking of Timeo, of everything that had happened, made her feel dizzy, and she forced herself to push it away. It had all happened ten years ago. A lifetime ago. A lifetime she'd never forget.

And a mistake she'd never make again…and certainly not with Rafe.

Straightening, Freya turned to face Rafe. He was watching her, his eyes narrowed, his head cocked, his gaze so thoroughly assessing.

Smoothing her skirt, Freya sat on the sofa across from him. 'Perhaps you should tell me a little bit about the arrangements in Spain.'

Rafe rolled the gold-plated fountain pen between his fingers; Freya's gaze was unwillingly yet unstoppably drawn to the small movement of those long, lean fingers.

'We will land in Madrid and spend a few days there. I have business to attend to. When it is taken care of I will take Max to my property in Andalusia.'

'And what is it like there? Is it accessible to a town? Will Max be able to attend nursery?'

Rafe frowned. 'I assume he will not. There is enough for him to get used to already.'

'I think it would help him settle,' Freya said firmly. 'Give him a routine, friends—'

'I'll look into it, Miss Clark.'

'Please, call me Freya. If we are to be living together—' She stopped abruptly, felt her cheeks redden with embarrassment. 'Sharing living space,' she amended, and Rafe's mouth quirked upwards. It was the first time she'd seen him smile.

'Don't worry,' he told her dryly. 'I took your meaning.'

Freya nodded stiffly, yet she could not keep a hot rush of awareness from coursing through her body and she shifted in her seat. Those innocent words had caused a reel of provocative images to flip through her mind—images of Rafe that had no business taking up space in her brain. Yes, he was a handsome, arresting, intimidating man, but she was *not* attracted to him. She couldn't be. She didn't do relationships, wasn't looking for a man. Didn't need or even deserve one, considering all that had happened before. And she could not afford the slightest slip when it came to caring for Max.

Rafe watched colour wash Freya's face, turn her eyes to smoke. Her tongue darted out and moistened her lower lip, and he experienced a sudden fierce jolt of lust. It surprised him because, while he hadn't been completely celibate since his divorce, he focused on business, not pleasure. Not desire. And yet now he felt it uncoil within him, and he could hardly credit that Freya Clark, with her neat ponytail and sensible shoes, was its source.

There was something unsettling about how still she kept herself, how those fog-coloured eyes gave nothing away. The fact that she was embarrassed by her silly slip of the tongue intrigued him, for Freya Clark seemed utterly in control of her emotions…if she had them at all. She felt passionately about staying with his son, he knew that, but it was still a careful, controlled ambition, and he knew that it was intentional—just like her expressionless face. Was it just a mask? What secrets and emotions could Freya Clark be hiding so carefully? For surely she was hiding something? Desire aside, his instinct told him not to trust her.

He capped his fountain pen and closed the folder of business documents that had been spread out on the table before him. 'How long have you been taking care of Max?'

'Three years.' She spoke firmly, clearly on familiar territory. 'Since he was three months old.'

Three years ago... That would have been less than a year after Rosalia had left him. She would have been four or five months pregnant; she would have known. And she'd never said. She had, in fact, told him the opposite. *I never mean to fall pregnant—ever.* Even now the memory sent a fresh rage rushing through him. He forced himself to relax.

'And how did you meet my ex-wife?'

'I answered an advert in a newspaper,' Freya replied. 'For a nanny. Rosalia's English wasn't exceptional, and she wanted someone who was fluent in Spanish to converse with her, but who could also teach her son English.' She lifted her shoulders in a shrug, the movement both delicate and graceful. 'I fit those requirements.'

Unusual requirements, Rafe thought. There were so many things he wanted to know: what Rosalia had said of him, how she had explained his absence. What lies she had told. And more, too, more about Freya herself: why was she a nanny? Why was she fluent in Spanish? *What was she hiding?*

For surely those clear grey eyes held some secrets.

'And have you been a professional nanny for very long?' he asked. 'Did you have a position before Max?' He supposed he should have asked for a reference before bringing her to Spain. He'd been so overwhelmed by meeting Max, by wanting to get him back to Spain—back *home*—that such considerations had completely slipped his mind. Still, he trusted Freya at least to care for Max. Beyond that...

Freya hesitated, causing Rafe to refocus, swinging his gaze back on her sharply. She bit her lip, looking unsure for only a second before she answered, 'I was a student before I cared for Max.'

'A student?' He'd assumed she was in her late twenties, simply based on the assured way she held herself. Despite that brief flash of uncertainty, Freya Clark had the composure and confidence of a woman, not a girl.

'Yes, I took am MPhil in pure mathematics,' she elaborated, although with seeming reluctance.

Rafe sat back, saying nothing. This woman had no end of surprises. She possessed an advance degree in an abstract and technical field, and yet she had been nannying for the last three years and seemed content—in fact, *intent*—on continuing to do so.

'And you did not wish to pursue a position in your field of study?'

Freya lifted her shoulders in a defensive shrug. 'No,' she said simply, and Rafe's gaze narrowed.

Something wasn't right. She was hiding something; he was sure of it now. She stared at him steadily, without a flicker or tremor, refusing to give anything away. Yet there was something silently defiant about that stare, and it told Rafe that Freya Clark was not telling him everything he needed to know. Or was he simply suspicious, because he wasn't used to taking women at face value? The two women he'd let into his heart—his mother and his wife—had both deceived him in the most devastating ways possible. Over and over again. He didn't trust Freya, but he didn't know if that was because of him...or her.

'What an interesting choice of study,' he finally said mildly. Was he imagining her relaxing, no more than the tiniest fraction of a movement, shoulders lowering, expression ironed out?

'It was,' Freya said in that same firm, cool voice. 'But caring for Max has been far more rewarding.'

'Indeed.' He steepled his fingers together, watched her over their tips. She'd tensed again; it was something he felt, as if they were connected by an invisible thread, a live wire. She didn't want to talk about herself, Rafe thought. She was afraid of revealing something—but what? 'And will you return to mathematics when your position here is finished?'

Pain flashed across her features, a lightning streak through her eyes before she composed herself again. Perhaps he had been needlessly cruel, reminding her that her position would end, but she needed to know it. He had no intention of Freya Clark staying around any longer than necessary.

'I'll have to see,' she told him, her voice and gaze both level. 'When the time comes.'

Max stirred then, letting out a little cry. Freya rose and went to him. Rafe watched her bending over the child, speaking in a low, soothing voice as she swept the silky dark hair from his forehead.

Watching her, the cheap material of her black skirt moulding itself over her hips, Rafe felt another lick of lust uncurl inside him, and he yanked his gaze away impatiently. His unexpected desire for Freya Clark was yet another reason to have her return to England as soon as possible.

CHAPTER FOUR

It was nearing midnight when they were finally driven to Rafe's home in Madrid. Freya hadn't really spoken to him again since that tense exchange on the aeroplane, and for that she could only feel relief. She didn't like the way Rafe looked at her—so assessing, *so knowing*. She saw suspicion in those dark eyes, and she wondered what he suspected. It wasn't as if she was hiding anything relevant from him. She had no secrets when it came to Max and her care of him. Yet still Rafe looked at her as if she did…and he intended on finding them out.

Max was exhausted from the flight, and he'd barely woken up as they'd left the plane. Freya had been bending to lift him when Rafe had stepped forward.

'Let me.'

Silently she had watched as he'd scooped his son into his arms, so gently that Max had barely stirred before nestling closer against Rafe—almost as if he instinctively recognised and trusted this stranger who had come so suddenly into his life.

The sight of Rafe cradling his son had made Freya's throat close up. This was how it was meant to be—parents and children. This was what she was missing out on being just Max's nanny. This was what she would forever miss out on.

She'd turned away, unable to watch, unwilling to feel…yet the pain and memory still lanced through her.

A limo had been waiting on the tarmac to take them into the city.

Freya breathed in the warm, sultry air, so different from the chill of early spring back in London. She remembered how she'd loved stepping into the sunshine when she'd flown into Barcelona ten years ago, her heart buoyant with the opportunities and possibilities ahead of her.

If only she'd known…

Would she have averted the heartbreak and loss that had come later? Could she have kept herself from that consuming despair? Or had the weaknesses which had led to so much heartache been there inside her, fault lines waiting to crack open and destroy everything she'd ever held dear?

Her gaze travelled to Rafe, the breadth of his shoulders, the darkness of his hair. Those fault lines were still there, she knew. Papered over, perhaps, but still visible. Still a threat. She had to be careful. Perhaps it was because he was Spanish, or simply because he was an unbearably handsome and charismatic man, but Rafe Sandoval presented her with a lethal temptation—and it was one she had to resist.

'Are you all right?' Rafe asked over Max's head. He was still holding his son, and Freya had slid into the seat next to them in the limo.

He must have felt her tension, sensed her anxiety. She forced herself to relax. Smile.

'I'm fine. Just a bit tired.'

Rafe nodded, accepting, and Freya turned her face to the window and watched the darkened streets slide by. Neither of them spoke, and Max didn't stir, yet the tension in the limo felt palpable—at least to Freya.

She was conscious of how close Rafe was sitting to her, his strong, muscled thigh just inches from her own, and how easily and gently he held Max. She could hear the steady sound of his breathing, could inhale the musk of his after-shave. All of it conspired to make her feel tense enough to snap. *Break.* There was simply too much about this whole situation that she didn't like. The rawness of old memories, the uncertainty of her present situation. Her unwanted attraction to Rafe Sandoval.

She took several slow, deep breaths, forced her fists to unclench even if her insides wouldn't.

'We're here.' The limo had pulled up to a stately building with ornamented pillars and portico, and a general aura of privilege and wealth. A liveried doorman opened the door.

'Señor Sandoval. *Buenas noches.*'

'Good evening,' Rafe returned in Spanish. 'Has my apartment been prepared?'

'Of course, *señor.*'

'*Bueno.*'

Rafe turned to his sleeping son, and in the wash of the streetlight Freya could see how his face softened, was suffused with tenderness. Her insides clenched again, this time with a nameless longing. She had not expected Rafe to seem so vulnerable when it came to his son. And so cold with her.

'Come, Max,' he whispered in Spanish. 'We are home now.'

Still holding Max, he slid out of the car and entered the building, leaving Freya no choice but to follow. She followed Rafe through an ornate foyer, its marble floor gleaming from the light of a crystal chandelier. Despite the late hour, several porters were in attendance, and they moved with quiet efficiency, taking their bags to a separate service lift. Freya followed Rafe into a wood-panelled lift, and the operator, also liveried, slid the iron grille in place before taking them to the top floor. The penthouse.

Freya glanced at Max, because it was better than looking at Rafe. She had to fight the insane impulse to look at him, to notice the hard angle of his jaw and the faint glint of stubble on his chin. The sound of him speaking Spanish, his voice low, the tone mellifluous, had slipped into her senses, stirred them to life. She'd forgotten what a beautiful language Spanish was—which was ridiculous, because she'd been speaking it to both Max and Rosalia for years. Yet somehow it was different when spoken by a man. By Rafe.

The operator slid the grille open, and Rafe walked straight into the penthouse flat. Clearly someone had been there cleaning, turning lights on, stocking the fridge. The place had an empty yet enlivened air, and Freya gazed at the stark, modern furniture, so at odds with the classical building and its stately architecture. Most of the interior walls had been taken out to create a huge open space, and long, sashed windows revealed Madrid in all its glittering glory.

Freya gazed in dismay at the leather-and-chrome sofas, the glass coffee table, the awkward sculptures of glass and iron that Max could so easily break or hurt himself on. This was hardly a place for a child.

Rafe must have realised that too, for he half turned to Freya, so his face was in profile, and said in a gruff whisper, 'We will leave as soon as possible for my house in Andalusia. It is much more suited for a child.' He jerked his head towards Max, still amazingly asleep, nestled against his father. 'I will put him to bed.'

'Of course.'

Until he left Freya hadn't realised they'd been speaking Spanish. She'd slipped into it so naturally. The thought caused her a ripple of foreboding. Being back in Spain was stirring up so many memories—memories of loss and desire and regret—and she did not want to feel them again. She didn't want to remember at all. She couldn't be tempted.

Alone in the huge reception room, she wandered around,

gazing at the sculpture and the modern art, wondering what it revealed about Rafe. The place felt stark and soulless, much like the man Rosalia had described.

'He never loved me. He never showed me any affection at all. How would he treat his child?'

Freya had listened to Rosalia's diatribes patiently, because she'd known how frazzled and fractured the other woman was; she'd never seemed comfortable or happy or even at peace. She'd never bonded with Max, despite Freya's attempts to bring them together. Freya had never known how much of Rosalia's misery was self-inflicted, and how much was caused by the man in the other room. The man putting his son to sleep so tenderly.

There was so much she hadn't expected, so much she didn't understand. She'd made assumptions about Rafe Sandoval based on what Rosalia had told her, what the media described, and yet when he looked at his son he seemed like someone else entirely. Someone kind and gentle and good.

'He seems to have settled,' Rafe said, startling her. She turned around, her arms folded in front of her in a posture of defence.

'Oh…good.'

Rafe propped one shoulder against the door, his gaze speculative.

'Your Spanish is very good.'

'I told you I was fluent.'

'Yes…and why *is* that?'

He arched one eyebrow, the low lighting from the lamps sending his face into half-shadow so Freya couldn't quite make out his expression. 'You are not Spanish.'

'My Spanish isn't that good?' Freya said wryly, surprising herself. At some point she must have mentally called a truce. This man was not her enemy. He showed too much concern for Max to be that. Yet he was still a danger.

'Not quite,' Rafe allowed.

Even in the shadowy light she saw a smile flicker across his face, and felt an answering tug of need deep in her belly. She took a step backwards.

'So how and why did you learn Spanish?'

'I studied it at school,' Freya said. She took a breath, knowing she would need to tell him more, that he would ask eventually. 'And I spent my gap year in Spain.'

'Gap year?'

'A year after sixth form,' Freya explained. 'When I was eighteen.'

The words felt like explosions in her heart, hollowing out holes. Ten years ago, and yet for a decade she'd acted as if that year didn't exist—hadn't happened. And here she was, admitting it to Rafe Sandoval. He'd slipped under her defences so easily, and she didn't even know how it had happened…or why. All she knew was that it was frightening and dangerous…and yet a part of her craved it at the same time—that closeness, an intimacy. She'd denied herself for so long, and yet she couldn't have picked a more inappropriate person to need. *Want.*

'Ah.' Rafe's gaze swept slowly over her, and Freya stared back coolly, refusing to look away or show any sign of weakness. 'You can sleep in the bedroom next to Max's,' Rafe finally said. 'Let me know if there is anything you need.'

Freya nodded, and he moved off to the other bedroom wing. Freya walked slowly down the corridor, peeking into a darkened room with its door ajar to see Max curled peacefully on a double bed.

In the room next door her bag had already been placed by the bed, although she hadn't noticed anyone enter the apartment besides themselves. Presumably there was a separate service entrance, and the staff were trained to come and go silently. She gazed around at all the opulence—the king-sized bed with its cream satin duvet, the plush carpet under her feet. She moved to the window and lifted the heavy damask drape; outside she saw a wrought-iron balcony, and she slid the door open to breathe in the dusky warm air.

Freya closed her eyes, letting the sultry breeze ripple over her. Happiness and sorrow warred within her. She was with Max. What more could she possibly want? Yet memories whispered on the fringes of her mind. Threatened to pull her under.

She'd known it would be difficult, returning to Spain after all these years, but she hadn't quite prepared herself for the way the very air brought her tumbling back to that old version of herself, innocent and untainted. She wished suddenly, fiercely, that she could go back and change the events of that year, erase the mistakes she'd made. She wished she could be a whole person—untroubled, unscarred—for Max. And maybe even for Rafe. If she was, would things be different now? Would she even be here at all? For surely it was her desperate knowledge that she could never have a child of her own that had derailed her mathematics career and led her to care for Max in the first place?

Freya undressed quickly, exhaustion not just from the flight but from the last week crashing over her in a wave, and slipped beneath the cool, slippery duvet. She fell asleep almost as soon as her head touched the pillow, despite the thoughts and memories churning through her mind and heart.

And she awoke to an unholy scream of terror renting the air.

CHAPTER FIVE

FREYA bolted out of bed, every nerve on high alert as the scream echoed through the apartment. It was coming, she knew, from Max. She recognised the sound of raw fear, for in the week since Rosalia had died he'd woken up several times with night terrors. She hurried out of her bedroom, stumbling in the unfamiliar surroundings, groping in the dark. And skidded to a halt on the threshold of Max's bedroom—for Rafe was already there.

She gaped in disorientated surprise as Rafe leaned over Max, whispering soothingly, stroking his hair. Max kept on screaming. His eyes were open, but Freya knew he wasn't really awake. She had yet to find a way to deal with Max's night terrors other than time and patience.

'What is wrong?' Rafe asked in a low voice. He did not take his gaze from his son. 'Why will he not stop? What can I do?'

There was a raw note of pleading in Rafe's voice that tore at Freya's heart. Rafe Sandoval was not a man used to being helpless.

'He's not really awake,' she said quietly. She moved to sit on the edge of the bed, next to Rafe. Too late she realised how few clothes either of them wore; Rafe was bare-chested, wearing only a pair of drawstring trousers, and because of the warm night she wore only a tank top and shorts. They were very close on the bed, their bare legs brushing, causing gooseflesh to rise all over Freya's body in an instinctive response of awareness.

She turned to Max, murmuring quietly, stroking his hair just as Rafe had. Now that the terror had run its course—or perhaps because Max recognised her, even in his sleep—he relaxed just a bit, his screams lowering to exhausted moans, and buried his head in Freya's lap.

'It's all right now, isn't it?' Freya said, her fingers sliding through his silky hair. 'You're all right, Max. It was nothing but a dream.'

Max jerked his head up, his unfocused eyes suddenly trained on Rafe. And he started screaming again.

Rafe tensed, and Freya said, a note of apology in her voice, 'He's asleep—he doesn't—'

'I'll go.' Rafe stood up and walked stiffly from the room. To Freya's dismay Max's screams subsided as soon as his father had left. The strange events of the day must have affected him on a subconscious level.

She stayed for a few more minutes as he dropped back into a deeper sleep, and then she tucked the blankets around him. She sat on the edge of the bed for a moment, wondering if she should go back to her own room. Had Rafe gone back to bed? He'd seemed almost hurt by his son's rejection, and that thought compelled her to tiptoe towards the living room.

Rafe stood by the window, a tumbler of whisky in his hand. He was still shirtless, and Freya could not keep herself from noticing how the moonlight slanting through the windows washed his body in silver, emphasising the sculpted muscles of his back, his broad shoulders and trim hips.

She almost turned around again and hightailed it back to her room, for her brain recognised that there was something dangerous about this situation—about both of them wearing almost nothing in the middle of the night, in a moon-washed room. Her body sensed danger too. Every nerve and sinew was singing to life, to a heightened awareness that was painful in its pleasure. It had been so long since she'd allowed herself to feel…anything.

'Why is he like that?' Rafe half turned to her, his face in profile.

Freya swallowed and stayed by the door. 'They're night terrors.'

'A dream?'

'Not exactly. More severe, I suppose, and harder to comfort because he never actually wakes up.'

'His eyes were open,' Rafe said in a low voice. 'He was looking at me as if…' He turned back to the window, not finishing the sentence. His throat worked, his pulse beating rapidly, a testament to his anger and fear.

'It wasn't you,' Freya said quickly, perhaps too quickly. She started towards him, stopping halfway across the room, aware that going nearer to Rafe right now might not be the best idea. The safest idea. 'He doesn't recognise anyone when he's like that.'

Rafe did not turn from the window. 'How long has he been having these terrors?'

'It's very common for children his age,' Freya said, knowing she was hedging. Why did she not want to tell Rafe? She knew the answer already; she didn't want to hurt him. Stupid, perhaps, and certainly impossible. Life was pain.

Rafe half turned to her again, and even from halfway across the room she saw the black glitter of his eyes. 'How long?'

'They've certainly been happening more often since Rosalia died,' she said quietly.

Rafe nodded, accepting. 'Of course. She was his mother.' His fingers clenched around his glass. 'Did she love him? Did she see him, hug him?'

Hug him. The question surprised Freya, and touched her too, for it seemed such a strangely specific and emotional thing for Rafe to be concerned about. Yet she understood the nature of the question, and she knew she had to answer truthfully. 'She loved him,' she said quietly, 'but she didn't see him that often.'

'How often?' Rafe asked in a raw voice, the question a demand.

'Once every few weeks?' Freya hazarded a guess. Towards the end it had been even less than that. If she was honest, at least with herself, Max had barely known his mother.

Rafe turned to her, shock and pain etched on his features. His chest rose and fell in a ragged breath, and Freya's gaze was helplessly drawn to the movement. 'Then you were his mother,' he said simply, 'in all but fact.'

Freya didn't speak for a moment; she couldn't. Too many emotions raced through her—hope and need and fear. She was glad Rafe could acknowledge how important she was to Max, and yet she was still dizzily afraid that he would force her to leave, that her closeness to Max would be a threat to his own relationship to his son. And she couldn't keep need from coiling within her at the sight of Rafe, at the very scent of him—the kind of hungry desire she hadn't felt in years. Hadn't let herself feel because she knew where it led. The misery and despair it could cause.

'Yes,' she finally said, in no more than a whisper, 'but it is a rather important fact.'

'Is it?' Rafe let out a bark of humourless laughter as he turned back to the window. 'Sometimes I wonder.'

Freya could not decipher that statement, or what had motivated it, but she heard the bleakness in Rafe's voice and knew its cause: three years of not knowing about his son, and now being faced with the seemingly insurmountable task of forging that all-important bond.

Impulsively she stepped towards him, going so far as to touch his arm. His skin was warm and the muscles jumped under her fingers. 'He'll get to know you,' she said. 'He'll come to love you. It just takes time.'

Rafe turned towards her, and Freya realised she had not taken her hand from his arm. Instead her fingers had stretched out along his skin, as if seeking the heat of him. She was standing so close to him, in nothing but a skimpy tank top and shorts, and her breath suddenly started coming fast—too fast. Desire overwhelmed her senses, her thoughts. She knew she should step away, yet she couldn't because she didn't want to. She wanted this, wanted Rafe, and even as the realisation shamed her—she was *still* weak—she could not keep it from overtaking her, from guiding her actions. Keeping her hand on his arm, sliding her fingers along his skin.

Rafe's face was still half turned to her, so she could see the strong line of his jaw, the fullness of his lips. And then he turned completely, his eyes glinting blackly in the moonlight, and he stared at her with a hunger that stole the breath from Freya's lungs. He wanted this, too. He wanted *her*. She didn't move.

The moment spun on—silent, taut with tension and yearning—and then with a whispered curse, Rafe closed the space between their bodies and kissed her.

The first feel of his lips against hers set off an explosion through Freya's body, obliterating the barriers she'd erected around her mind, her heart. She wasn't prepared for her sudden intense reaction; she had no defence. Her mouth opened under his and her arms came up to grip his shoulders, although whether to push him away or pull him closer she did not know. Perhaps she simply needed to anchor herself.

She felt tension shudder through Rafe, and knew he'd been surprised by her response. He'd expected her to push him away. Of course he had; it was what she should have done. Yet now that he'd kissed her she could not keep herself from wanting this, wanting more, craving closeness, needing the connection. It had been so long. It had been ten years.

His mouth stilled over hers, the taste of him still on her lips, and she knew he was battling with himself. Knowing he should stop. One of them should step away. And yet even in this moment, as cold rationality seeped through her mind, she could not control the craving, and her hands tightened on his shoulders.

It amazed and shamed her that after ten years of holding herself apart, keeping herself numb and distant and totally under control, this one man, in one moment, had completely conquered her. Overcome her defences. Awoken her emotions. Reminded her of her own weakness.

The moment broke and Rafe's mouth took sure possession of hers once more. Freya completely lost all power of thought. All power, full-stop. She could do nothing but respond, *need*, even if it made her weak. Again.

Rafe slid his hands to her shoulders, bracing her, before moving them to the hem of her tank top, and then underneath, sliding along her skin. The intimate contact overwhelmed her utterly. She stumbled back, needing the anchor of his hands, and he moved with her until her backside came into contact with a marble-topped table, the edge cold and hard against her.

In one fluid movement Rafe hoisted her so she sat on top of the table, and out of instinct and pure need she wrapped her legs around his waist, pulling him closer so they were—almost—in the most intimate contact possible. There could be no mistaking her intent...or his.

Rafe's breathing was ragged as he continued to kiss her with a pent-up passion and fury that Freya's body echoed and gave back to him. His tongue delved into her mouth time and time again and she felt the scrape of stubble on her cheek, the softness of his lips against hers, the glorious hardness of his body against hers, pressing, insistent.

Rafe did not break the kiss as he pulled at the waistband of her shorts, pushing them down, and Freya helped him, knowing this was moving crazily fast and yet powerless to stop it. Not wanting to.

His hand shook as he pulled at the waistband of his own pyjama bottoms, and then kicked them off. And then suddenly, amazingly, he was inside her. Freya gasped at the feeling; her body closed around him, tight and unused to the sensation, the sense of fullness and completion.

He muttered an oath, the words no more than a hiss, as he began to move. Freya moved with him, her face buried in the hot curve of his shoulder, tasting the salt of his skin. Or perhaps it was her own tears, because belatedly, distantly, she realised she was crying.

And then release came for both of them—an intense wave of emotion and pleasure that crashed over them, leaving them shuddering, silent and senseless.

His breathing still ragged, his chest heaving, Rafe remained in the circle of her arms, still inside her, for one precious beat, before he pulled away, yanked up his trousers and left the room.

CHAPTER SIX

RAFE stalked into his room, dazed and shaking. *What had just happened?*

He took a shuddering breath and raked a hand through his sweat-dampened hair. He knew all too well what had happened. He just couldn't believe he had done it. It seemed utterly impossible that he had just had sex with Freya Clark, yet he felt satiation stealing through his body even as his mind rebelled, denied. He had known her for less than twenty-four hours. He had had no intention of so much as laying a finger on her. And yet within minutes—seconds— all that had changed.

She had come close to him and he'd breathed in the faint scent of lilac that he knew must be from her soap or shampoo, seen the rise and fall of her chest through her thin tank top as she breathed, and he had felt a sudden, desperate tidal wave of yearning that he hadn't been able to control.

And when she had responded in kind…her mouth opening under his, accepting, *wanting*…that tidal wave had dragged him under completely.

After four long, lonely years—years of living off anger and bitterness rather than desire or love—he'd wanted that immediate connection and satisfaction, had needed it from *her*, and that deep need had overtaken any reason or self-control he'd had. The thought shamed him.

And now he was left with the aftermath of that rash act. How could they go forward with that between them? How could they concentrate on Max? He would have to tackle it directly, Rafe knew, yet he could not face it now. The realisation shamed him further. He'd shown such appalling weakness. He shuddered, shook off the thought.

He would speak to Freya in the morning. Explain—what? That it shouldn't have happened? He knew she would agree. Surely she hadn't expected...

Had she *planned* it? Rafe stilled, his body tensing with sudden suspicion. Had Freya been trying to seduce him as a way to bind herself closer to Max, keep him from finding another care-giver? The suspicions slid slyly into Rafe's mind, causing him to freeze as he considered the awful possibility. He thought of how she'd placed her hand on his arm, how she hadn't moved it. She'd looked up at him, her eyes wide, her mouth parted, *waiting*, and then her shocking, shameless response...

Had she used him?

God knew he had little reason to trust Freya Clark. He'd felt she was hiding something from the start—sensed that calm composure was covering some purpose or plan—but *seduction*? Did she really think a single night of rushed pleasure would change his mind? And yet in that moment of shocking intimacy he'd felt closer to Freya Clark than he had to another human being in a long, long time. She could not have expected him to respond that way, to have known how much he longed for it.

And yet it had happened. Freya had approached him, had not turned away from his kiss despite his every expectation that she would. Rafe's mouth twisted in disgust at both her and himself even as he fought against the urge to condemn her without true proof. He did not want to be unjust, yet he'd faced so much injustice himself.

And even if she *had* been using him, he could not send her away so suddenly. Max would be devastated. He thought of Max's blankly terrified face, the endless screams. Max needed Freya—for several more weeks, at least. They were stuck together, at least for a little while, no matter what her intentions had been. He didn't trust her. And he still had every intention of sending her away as soon as possible.

Freya walked from the living room as if she were made of glass. She felt as if she could shatter at any moment. She walked with her arms wrapped around herself, as if she could keep herself together by sheer physical force.

How could she have allowed herself to be so weak, tempted by desire yet again? How could ten years of distance and decorum, of carefully building a fortress around her body and heart, count for nothing? She felt as defenceless as a razed tower, her body and heart raw and vulnerable, open and exposed to the elements. To Rafe.

She thought of how he'd left the room, stalking from it as if he were angry, probably disgusted. By what they had done. By *her*. Had he sensed that weakness inside her? Had he known she would respond to his kiss, unable to keep desire from swamping her senses, obliterating all reason?

Freya went to the bathroom and, mindless of the late hour, ran a steaming bath. She needed to wash away the memory of what had just happened even if she couldn't erase the regret. She would, Freya knew from experience, live with that for ever.

Even after a bath, sleep wouldn't come. She kept reliving those urgent moments with Rafe—the feel of his lips on her skin, his body inside her, the fierce sense of both joy and regret, pleasure and pain. She had not been close, much less had sex, with anyone for ten years. Since Timeo. And it stunned and scared her that Rafe Sandoval had been the one to crumble her defences. She turned her head towards her pillow, closing her eyes tightly, willing the memories and regrets to recede.

She must have slept, although she did not remember doing so, for she opened her eyes several hours later to see Max standing very close to her face, peering owlishly at her. Freya blinked and tried to smile, although every muscle in her body ached.

'Hello, there, sleepyhead.'

Max grinned. 'You're the sleepyhead.'

'So I am.' She touched his cheek, as soft and round as a peach, savouring the moment. Then the memories of last night rushed in, obliterating anything else, crashing over her so her throat closed up and her eyes stung. She withdrew her hand. 'Let me just get dressed, Max, and we'll go and see about breakfast.'

A few minutes later, with Max's hand slipped through her own, Freya cautiously headed out into the apartment. Rafe was nowhere to be seen, and she felt a dizzying wave of relief. She wasn't ready to see him yet; she didn't know if she ever would be.

A housekeeper was busy in the kitchen, setting out bowls of fruit and slices of warm bread with pots of butter and jam, and she smiled at both Freya and Max as they entered. Freya made introductions, and they sat down at a table in the alcove and set to eating.

'How long are we going to stay here?' Max asked as he popped a strawberry in his mouth, juice running down his chin.

'I'm not sure, Max. I think we'll see Rafe's house in the country soon. Wouldn't you like that? To visit the mountains?'

Max frowned, and Freya knew she hadn't fooled him. Despite her cheerful, brisk attitude, he sensed that something wasn't right about this whole scenario.

'I want to go swimming,' he finally said, and Freya knew he was remembering Rafe mentioning that he had a pool.

'And you will. It's warmer in Spain, you know. You can go swimming outside even this time of year.'

Max brightened at this, and turned back to his fruit. Freya felt another wave of relief. She wasn't ready to offer Max explanations she couldn't even give. Thank goodness children were resilient.

Certainly more resilient than she was… She felt fragile and bruised, her body and brain both aching with the aftermath of last night.

Even as those thoughts ricocheted through her mind Rafe entered the kitchen. He was dressed for work, looking cool and remote in an immaculately cut business suit, a gold and silver watch flashing on one wrist. He greeted Maria, the housekeeper, and accepted a cup of coffee before turning to the two of them at the table.

'Good morning, Maximo.' His face softened in a smile clearly meant only for his son. He did not look at Freya. Max grinned back, his face and shirt already splotched with strawberry stains. 'I'm afraid I must be at work today, but tomorrow we will go to my house in Andalusia and have fun there. *Bueno*?'

Max nodded shyly. *'Bueno,'* he said.

Then Rafe turned to her, his mouth tightening, his eyes narrowing. The movements were almost imperceptible, yet Freya saw them. Felt them. He looked angry, she realised with a shaft of pain that surprised her, even though she should have expected it. He was blaming her—just as she couldn't keep from blaming herself. 'We will talk tonight.'

She nodded, returning his gaze, refusing to allow all the aching emotion to show on her face. She might have suffered a moment of weakness in allowing Rafe access to her body, but she would never let him into her mind or heart. That would be even more dangerous, more painful.

Rafe stared at her, his gaze still narrowed, as if he was trying to understand her…and then make a judgement. Then, after a tense pause, he turned away, and Freya let out the breath she hadn't realised she'd been holding.

After breakfast Freya took Max for a walk in the neighbourhood, Barrio Salamanca. They window-shopped on the chic Calle Serrano, and gazed at the modern sculptures—much like the ones in Rafe's apartment—at the Museo de Escultura Abstracta.

By lunchtime Max was worn out, and Freya tucked him in for a nap before lying down herself, since she'd got very little sleep last night. Her body still thrummed with memories, ached with regret. Her mind insisted on replaying every moment with Rafe, and despite his coolness this morning she realised that she still desired him. At least her body did. Her body longed for his touch again.

She managed a restless doze before Max woke up, and then they ate a light dinner that Maria had prepared. Rafe still wasn't home by the time Freya had bathed Max and tucked him into bed with several of his favourite stories.

'When will Rafe come back?' he asked, after she'd read each story at least twice. His eyes were already drooping and his thumb hovered near his mouth.

'Tonight,' Freya promised. 'And tomorrow we will go to his other house.'

'With the pool?'

'With the pool,' Freya confirmed, glad it could be—at least for now—that simple for Max.

She stayed until his eyes fluttered closed and his breathing evened out. In the distance she heard a door open and close, and she knew from the sound—and the plunging sensation in her middle—that Rafe had returned.

Of course she couldn't avoid him for ever, yet she still dreaded seeing him—had no idea how to handle the moment his coldly assessing gaze met hers.

She stood on the threshold of the living room, watching as Rafe shrugged out of his suit jacket and loosened the knot of his tie. Then he turned to face her, and the very air seemed to freeze. Freya's mind blanked so she could only stare at him, remember how she'd buried her face in his shoulder, wrapped her legs around his waist. Cried in his arms.

'Max is asleep?'

Freya nodded. She did not trust herself to speak.

Rafe took a breath and let it out slowly. 'Last night…'

She waited, tensing, knowing she should rush in and fill that silence with words and explanations, but she couldn't. She'd had plenty of time today to attempt to formulate a coherent reason for what had happened last night, how the darkness and memories and intensity of Max's terror had conspired to create an impossible, uncontrollable urge in both of them, yet now that seemed just a flimsy excuse for something that had—at least for her—been far deeper, darker, and more damaging. So she simply stared, and watched Rafe's expression flatten and harden, the suspicion and anger flaring in his eyes.

'It should not have happened,' he said after a long, tense moment. 'At least I did not intend for such a thing.'

The slight stress on *I* made Freya stiffen. 'I didn't either,' she answered, her voice thankfully cool.

Rafe glanced at her sharply. 'Didn't you?' he said, and Freya recoiled. So he *was* going to blame her. The realisation did not really surprise her, but it still hurt.

'Is that what you think?' she asked levelly. 'That I seduced you?'

Rafe let out a short huff of sound—something torn be-

tween laughter and despair. He hunched one shoulder. 'God
knows what I think,' he said in a low voice.

Freya sagged slightly in relief. She'd been expecting accusations, harsh and unrelenting. *You should know better. What
kind of girl are you?* Things she'd heard and endured before.
And yet despite Rafe's admission she still felt guilty. She
wondered if she would ever be free of that old guilt—that
fear—if any relationship she had would be untainted by it.
Its leaden weight was why she'd avoided relationships of any
kind for so long, and yet somehow with Rafe she'd forgotten.
At least for a moment.

And yet that she'd forgotten at all made her feel guiltier
than ever.

Rafe gazed at her thoughtfully, his eyes narrowing once
more, and Freya felt as if he could see into her soul. Sense
her guilt. 'Did I…hurt you?' he finally asked, his voice low.

His gaze remained steady on her, colour high on his
cheekbones, and Freya looked away. His thoughtfulness
both touched and shamed her. The encounter had been so
explosive, so urgent; clearly it had shocked him as much as
her.

'No,' she whispered. Not unless she counted the pain in
her heart.

Rafe nodded, accepting. 'I must ask,' he continued, his
voice still low. 'Is there any chance you could be pregnant?'

Shock raced through Freya, icy and unpleasant. She had
not considered that Rafe would think of such a thing. 'No,'
she said, her voice even lower than his, barely audible. 'There
isn't.'

'You are on birth control?'

She flushed and looked away. 'It's taken care of.'

Rafe gazed at her, and Freya felt the weight of his stare.
No doubt he was wondering just what that meant. Was she on

the Pill? Had she taken emergency contraception? She gave him no answers.

'That's good, then,' he finally said, although he still sounded suspicious. 'Tomorrow we will travel to my house in Andalusia. Max should get settled there as soon as possible.'

Freya nodded, knowing what he was implying. *Settled so you can leave.* Her hands clenched, fingers curling into her palms. She forced herself to flatten them out, seem calm. Memories ricocheted through her.

Is there any chance you could be pregnant?

No. Never.

The pain of that old loss was magnified by the knowledge that she would lose Max too—in a matter of weeks, maybe months.

Rafe let out a tiny sigh, and Freya couldn't tell if he was sorrowful or just exasperated. 'We will put this behind us,' he said.

Freya nodded mechanically. She agreed with him completely, in the rational part of her mind, at least, yet she knew how difficult it could be to put mistakes behind you. Sometimes the only way to do it was to pretend it hadn't happened at all.

Yet now, with Rafe, she wondered if that was even possible.

CHAPTER SEVEN

'LOOK, Freya!'

Freya shielded her eyes from the sun as Max jumped into the shallow end of the pool. He squealed in delight as he hit the water, and she clapped her hands. '*Fantástico*, Max!' They had spoken only Spanish since arriving at Rafe's villa in Andalusia, and Max had accepted it naturally—just as he had accepted everything about his surroundings.

And why shouldn't he? It was paradise, after all. Stretched out on a sun lounger, Freya gazed around at the pool, fringed by palm and orange trees, with the rocky, barren mountains a stunning backdrop to the villa's extensive gardens and grounds. In the three weeks since they'd been there Max had been content to swim and play, to explore the gardens and walk down the dusty country road to a nearby farm where they had just had a litter of kittens.

Rafe had stocked his villa with a variety of shiny new toys and books, and outfitted a bedroom as a nursery, with child-sized beds, tables and chairs. Max had everything he could possibly want. He didn't even ask about England any more, or his mother. He'd adapted to his surroundings, and to Rafe, with childlike ease and joy.

Freya knew she should be glad he'd adjusted so well. And she was. Yet still she still felt uneasy, restless, because she did not know how long this would last. How long *she* would last. Every day she waited for Rafe to inform her she was no longer needed.

Rafe had been telecommuting with his office from the villa these last three weeks, with just a few short overnight trips to Madrid. He always made sure to spend time with Max, stopping by the pool or the nursery, and every afternoon playing with Max or reading him a story while Freya made herself scarce by silent agreement. The sight of their dark heads bent together sent a pang through her, a shaft of longing she had no right to feel.

Rafe had been cordial to her these last weeks, and they'd had a few careful conversations. Still, Freya felt as if they were orbiting around each other—Max the pull of gravity that kept them on similar but separate courses. Even so, his presence, his gentleness with his son, the way he'd tousle Max's hair with a look of longing on his face—all of it made her wish things were different. *She* was different.

She didn't let herself daydream beyond that vague thought, for she knew it was too dangerous. The kind of encounter she'd experienced with Rafe was surely nothing to build a relationship on—even if that were something either of them wanted. Which of course it wasn't.

Yet despite the distance they maintained she couldn't keep herself from watching Rafe as he spoke with Max, from noticing the almost reddish gleam in his dark hair, the easy grace with which he crouched down to talk to Max. Laughter rang through the house when they were playing together, surprising her because she'd never heard Rafe laugh before, and the sound made her ache. This man was not what she'd expected, what Rosalia had told her he was. At least not with Max.

With *her*...

'*Buenas tardes.*'

Rafe strolled into the pool area, looking cool and casual

in a loose white shirt and tan trousers. His feet were bare and tanned, his manner relaxed as he smiled at Max. Freya's insides clenched with a nameless longing.

'You are turning into a fish, Max,' Rafe said. 'Where are your fins?'

Max splashed in the shallows, grinning. 'I don't have fins!'

Rafe crouched down by the side of the pool, a smile softening his features, making him look entirely too approachable. Too wonderful. 'No? Are you sure?'

Max continued to splash about, and slowly, as if he needed to steel himself, Rafe turned to Freya. 'You are well?' he enquired politely.

'Very well,' Freya replied, just as politely. She hated how artificial they were with each other, yet she did not know how to change it. She doubted Rafe even wanted to. And she had no intention of boring him with the truth—which was that over the past few days she'd felt a little off…tired and nauseous. It was no doubt some kind of bug, and she'd get over it without any help from Rafe.

'Damita has prepared lunch,' Rafe told her. 'A seafood paella. Are you ready to eat?'

Freya couldn't quite keep from making a face. Although the housekeeper made delicious meals, the thought of seafood put her right off.

Rafe raised his eyebrows. 'Does that not suit you?' he asked mildly.

'I'm sorry. I have been feeling a bit nauseous these past few days. Probably some sort of stomach bug.' She swung her legs off the lounger and turned to Max, intending to call him out of the water.

'Nauseous?' Rafe repeated. 'How long has this been going on?'

'A few days, that is all. It goes away by dinnertime.'

Rafe had stilled, tensed.

'If you are worried that it might interfere with my care of Max—'

'No,' he said softly. 'I am not concerned about that.'

He paused, and Freya saw him looking at her with that narrow, assessing gaze that had been thankfully absent these past few weeks. He looked suspicious—but of what? A bout of stomach flu? Uneasily she turned back to Max.

'Max, get out of the water. It is time for lunch.' She waited for Rafe to say something, but he remained standing there, silent, as Max scrambled from the pool, and Freya held up a towel, bundling him into it with a smile and a ruffle of his wet hair.

It could not be. Surely it could not be. Rafe watched Freya as she dried off Max, cuddling him a bit, and his insides tightened.

Nauseous. Tired. He knew the signs; God only knew he'd been looking for them for the five years of his marriage— hoping, praying that Rosalia would fall pregnant, that they would have a family. The family he'd always wanted. The family he'd never had as a child.

Their marriage had ended when she'd revealed to him that it hadn't been possible, that she'd never *wanted* it to be possible. With a flash of ever-present anger Rafe remembered the swamping sense of betrayal, the hollow sensation of realising he'd been waiting and hoping in utter futility.

Yet even that had been a lie. Had Rosalia *ever* told him the truth? Had any woman?

And was Freya lying to him now? Had she lied to him when she told him it was 'taken care of'?

Could she be pregnant?

Rafe turned away from the sight of her, her dark red hair falling forward to hide her face as she towelled Max dry. In the heat she wore just a tee shirt and shorts, and he could see the curve of her shoulder, the thin fabric pulling taut over the bone. Even that simple sight caused desire to tug deep inside his belly. Was he imagining that her curves were looking lusher and fuller?

He'd spent the last three weeks trying not to notice her, trying to ignore the lust that fired his body and something different and deeper that touched his heart. Although he pretended not to notice, he couldn't quite keep his gaze from her as she played with Max, or read him a story, her lovely features softened and suffused with love. He'd fully intended packing Freya back off to England by now, yet when he saw the bond she shared with his son he knew he could not—and not just for Max's sake. Not even for Freya's.

For his own.

Despite the distance they'd silently agreed to maintain, he was not ready for Freya to leave. It was unreasonable—idiotic, even—yet it was there all the same: a deep and desperate need for a woman he knew was completely off-limits. And who might be pregnant with his child.

'Come along, Max,' he said, his voice coming out a little rougher than he'd intended. The thought that Freya might be pregnant, might *know* she was pregnant, made fury pulse through him. Lied to. *Again.*

He didn't talk to Freya until that evening, when Max was settled in bed. He waited outside the doorway until she'd said goodnight and clicked off the light. 'I need to talk to you.'

Freya gasped aloud, one hand flying to her chest. 'Oh! You startled me.'

He watched colour flare in her face, her grey eyes wide, and realised he hardly ever saw her discomfited or surprised or anything but coolly rational. Perhaps that was why her response in his arms had been so unsettling and explosive. It had not been at all expected.

'I'm sorry,' he said. 'Do you have a moment?' He'd adopted that cool, polite voice, and Freya took it as her cue to match it.

'Yes, of course.' She followed him downstairs into the living room. The room was huge and formal and Rafe hardly ever used it.

He paced to the window, conscious of her standing in the doorway, slight and uncertain.

'Is something wrong?' she finally asked.

'I don't know,' Rafe said. He'd wanted to sound calm, measured, but he heard coldness and even anger creeping in. *You tricked me. Betrayed me.* The accusations clamoured in his throat. Would he ever know a woman who was honest? Yet even now, as he turned to face her, saw her eyes widen and her face pale, he wanted to trust her. Stupidly, perhaps, but he could not deny that basic craving.

He saw Freya swallow, lift her chin. 'Is there something you want to say?' she asked evenly, and despite her level tone he knew she was frightened—saw the pulse flutter in her throat.

What was she afraid of? What was she hiding? If she knew she was pregnant, surely she would tell him, trap him? Keeping it from him—just as Rosalia had—made no sense. Rosalia had acted out of spite and hurt, but surely Freya did not harbour such motives? For a moment Rosalia's last words to him rang through his head, obliterating all rational thought:

'I never intended to fall pregnant. I've been on the Pill, Rafe, since our honeymoon. I don't want your baby.'

'Rafe?' Freya spoke quietly, her forehead furrowing in concern.

Rafe let out a slow breath, forced the memories to recede. Freya was not Rosalia. He still didn't trust her, didn't know what secrets she hid, but she was not his ex-wife. She was not, please God, deceiving him the way his ex-wife had. She might not even be pregnant. A little nausea could be explained away, surely? He was simply being overly alert. Paranoid.

Hopeful.

The word caught him on the raw. Did he *want* another child? The child of this near-stranger? The thought made no sense, yet he could not keep that tiny tendril of hope—or something close to it—from unfurling inside him. He'd wanted a family for so long—had dreamed of the day he would have a child, a wife. And now he found he could picture Freya as a mother all too easily, her slender arms cradling a baby—their baby. With a jolt he realised he did not want just the child, the way he had with Rosalia. He wanted the woman too.

Freya.

What was it about this woman that called out to him, made him want in a way he never had before? Made him *feel* in a way he never had before? Was it the glimpse of passion underneath that cool exterior? Or the gentleness and kindness she showed to Max? Or was it simply the whole person—beautiful, alluring, kind, *secretive*?

He still didn't know what secrets she hid.

Freya simply stared at him, her face pale and beautiful, her eyes wide. She looked heartrendingly beautiful.

'Freya,' he said, and when she blinked in surprise he realised it was the first time he'd used her Christian name. 'Have you considered that you might be pregnant?'

CHAPTER EIGHT

'PREGNANT?' Freya repeated numbly, for of course the possibility had never once—not even remotely—crossed her mind. She shook her head, suppressing the sudden, bizarre blaze of hope Rafe's words had caused to streak through her. 'No.'

Impatience flashed across his features. 'Why not?'

'It's impossible,' Freya told him flatly. It hurt to say it.

Rafe shook his head, nonplussed.

'I'm infertile,' she elaborated. His expression did not change.

'Are you certain?'

Anger spiked through her, firing her words. 'Am I *certain*?' she repeated, her voice rising, giving way to the ocean of emotion underneath. She strove to temper it, to keep herself as calm and remote as always. She could not give in to the emotions and memories now. If she did, she might drown in them. 'Of course I am.'

Rafe shrugged. 'It is perhaps possible, though?'

'No, it isn't,' Freya said coldly. She hated that he was pressing her, giving her hope. She'd lived with her infertility for ten years. Had accepted it…almost.

Perhaps this is your punishment. A girl like you…

'It is not possible. And I'm surprised you'd even think of it, based on such little evidence. A little nausea—'

His mouth compressed into a thin line. 'I looked for pregnancy symptoms in my wife for five years. I know the signs.'

His admission caused shock to slice through her. Five years? 'And she never fell pregnant?'

'No,' Rafe told her flatly. 'Because she was on the Pill the entire time and didn't tell me. She never wanted children, even though I—' He stopped, his lips pressed firmly together, his body taut with suppressed emotion.

'But then she did become pregnant, and kept it from you?' Freya filled in slowly.

'Exactly.' Rafe turned back to her with a grim smile. 'By accident, I must suppose. She deceived me twice—first by taking birth control when she knew how much I wanted a child, and then by keeping her pregnancy secret from me.'

'I suppose I can understand why you wanted a paternity test,' Freya said quietly, and Rafe's features twisted.

'I did not realise she hated me so much.' He raked a hand through his hair, then let it fall. 'I think you should take a pregnancy test. Just in case.'

'It's not—'

'I know,' he cut across her. 'But at least it will rule out the possibility.'

This was what Rosalia lived with for five years, Freya supposed. The pressure, the tension, and then of course his disappointment. By the time Freya had met her Rosalia had surely hated Rafe. Yet what had caused that hate? Five years of expectation and disappointment could not have helped. Had she ever loved him? Freya thought she must have. Her hatred had seemed fuelled by disappointment and despair. Had Rafe ever loved his wife, Freya wondered, or just the idea of a child?

'I'll buy a test tomorrow,' Rafe told her.

Freya shrugged her acceptance. If it eased Rafe's mind, she would take the test. She knew what the result would be.

* * *

Positive. Two pink lines. Freya sat on the edge of the bath and stared disbelievingly at the test stick. It couldn't be. It was impossible. She knew it was.

Yet the evidence was right there in her hand—two blazing pink lines that meant she was pregnant. She scrabbled for the leaflet that had come with the test, checked again. Yes. Pregnant. And what about false positives? *Very rare,* the leaflet said.

And yet…

It couldn't be.

Even so an incredulous hope was filling her up inside, buoying her heart. She felt a sudden fierce joy—a joy she'd never thought to experience. A child. *Her* child. A miracle.

'Freya?' Rafe stood outside the bathroom door, impatience sharpening his voice.

The disbelieving joy of seeing the test results gave way to a greater shock. She was pregnant…with Rafe's child. It was a miracle, but it was also a mess.

'Just a minute.' From somewhere Freya found her voice. Fumbling with the lock, she opened the bathroom door. She had no words—she felt suddenly near tears—so she simply handed the test stick to Rafe. He took it automatically, then stared down at those two lines.

For a split second, no more, Freya thought he looked almost—*happy.* He didn't smile, but his features softened in a way that made her yearn for this moment to be so different from what it was. Then his expression was ironed out and he tossed the stick in the bin.

'You're pregnant.' He spoke levelly, without any inflection.

Freya nodded. 'Yes, it would seem… I thought it was impossible. I was sure…'

'Were you?' Rafe enquired coolly.

Freya's gaze flew to his face. She saw his eyes had narrowed, his lips pursed. She was starting to know that look so well.

'What are you suggesting?' she asked, her voice as cool as his. 'That I tricked you somehow? That I planned what—what happened and thought I might get pregnant that one time? You still suspect some kind of *seduction*?' Even though she kept her voice level and expressionless, she knew Rafe could hear the scorn.

'I don't know what to think,' he said evenly. 'You told me it was taken care of. I assumed you were on birth control—'

'I am *infertile*.' Freya cut across him, the words raw and wounded. 'I was told I was infertile. I had no reason to doubt it.' She swallowed convulsively, unable to say more. Rafe's narrow gaze took in her sudden silence, and she knew he was not satisfied with her answer.

He nodded towards her still-flat belly. 'Obviously the person who told you was mistaken.'

Freya placed her hand on her middle, as if she could somehow sense the tiny life within. *Pregnant.* A child. A chance she'd never, ever thought to have. Rafe raised his eyebrows, and suddenly, fiercely, Freya said, 'I'm keeping it.'

Rafe drew back, clearly startled by the fierceness of her tone. 'I was not suggesting otherwise.'

'Good.' She let out a harsh breath. 'This baby is a miracle. I never thought I'd fall pregnant.' Repercussions were slamming through her mind. This baby was not hers alone. 'You've said you wanted children...' she began hesitantly, not even sure what point she meant to make.

Rafe's mouth thinned. 'I have a child.'

The words hurt even as Freya lifted her chin. 'Fine. If you think I'm asking for help, or money, or something like that—'

'I don't know what you want.' Rafe cut across her, his tone suddenly savage. 'I've never known what you wanted.' He took a step closer to her, the action seeming both menacing and desperate. His eyes flashed blackly. 'But I know you are hiding something from me, and when I find out what it is…'

It wasn't quite a threat, but close enough that Freya felt a shiver steal straight through her, all the way to her soul.

'Whatever secrets I have,' she whispered, 'have nothing to do with you.'

Rafe's mouth curved in a humourless smile. 'I knew from the moment I met you that you were hiding something from me. You still are. I've been deceived enough before to know the signs.'

Freya felt her heart start to beat with fast, fearful thuds. She could not deny that she was hiding something; she'd been hiding something for ten years. Yet neither could she confess. The thought of facing Rafe's sure scorn and disgust was more than she could bear. Besides, it was her secret and hers alone. It had nothing to do with their baby.

Their baby.

'I think you must be paranoid,' she told him coolly. 'I am not Rosalia. I am not lying to you. I genuinely believed myself to be infertile.'

'I believe you,' Rafe returned, yet his tone suggested that was just about all he believed.

Freya could not keep herself from looking away, and Rafe noticed.

His mouth thinned once more. 'I will make an appointment at the doctor's in Seville.'

Freya swallowed. Tasted bile. Memories came rushing back—memories of pregnancy tests and doctors' offices, of disappointment and despair. She'd been eighteen years old, alone in Barcelona. It had been different, and yet so much the same. She looked away, blinking hard.

'What is wrong?' Rafe asked.

Freya drew in a deep breath. She could not let memories claim her now—not when Rafe was already so suspicious.

'Nothing. That is…this is a lot to take in.'

'So it is.' Rafe paused, and Freya tensed. He looked so serious, and so very determined. 'If the doctor confirms this pregnancy, and it is viable,' he said, his gaze dark and steady, 'you will marry me.'

Even though she'd strangely half expected it, Freya still felt an icy ripple of shock douse her senses. 'That isn't the only solution.'

'It is for me.'

She raised her chin. 'You want to get married after your first experience?'

He flinched, and she realised she'd hurt him. 'At least with this marriage we'll both go in knowing the circumstances—and the limitations.'

'Which are?'

'It will be a marriage of convenience—one that is best for the child.'

He made it sound so simple, Freya thought. So obvious. 'And a loveless business arrangement is best for a child?' she asked, a revealing catch in her voice.

'Knowing both your parents is best for a child,' Rafe returned harshly.

'That doesn't require marriage—'

'My child will *not* grow up a bastard.' She flinched, and he gave a hollow laugh. 'I would not wish that on any child. I'm speaking from experience.'

Her mouth dropped open. *'You—'*

Rafe slashed a hand through the air. 'Marriage is the only option.'

Freya felt a hollow sensation in her chest, as if she had emptied out. She had not expected such a demand so soon, so suddenly. 'And if I don't agree?'

'Don't go there, Freya.'

The words were a warning, given with the kind of cold control that reminded her she was speaking to El Tiburón. The shark of the business world who devoured what he wanted and discarded what he didn't. And right now, Freya thought, he wanted her child.

He didn't want *her*. Not the way she wanted to be wanted, anyway. To be cherished, loved. Not that she'd even dared to hope for it, but to sign her entire life away to a man who didn't love her, didn't trust her—

A man who was gentle with his child, whose smile made her ache. A man whom she knew, terrifyingly, she could fall in love with if she let herself. And who would never love her.

'Are you threatening me?' she asked, her voice still thankfully level and even cool.

'See it as you like,' Rafe replied. 'You are carrying my child. I missed the first three years of my son's life. If you think I am going to allow—'

'And if I refuse?'

'Then I will do everything in my power to ensure I retain custody,' Rafe said.

The words fell like stones into the silence, creating irrevocable ripples. They were words that could not be unsaid, with implications Freya did not want to envisage.

She swallowed, pushed past the bitterness and bile that crowded her throat. She'd thought Rafe was a good, gentle man, and he was—with Max. With her he was something else entirely. With her he was El Tiburón. Was this what Rosalia had faced? This heartless ambition, this single-minded determination to provide and care for his child? Was this why she had stopped loving him? Why she had left?

'Why?' she asked when she finally trusted her voice. 'Why would you threaten to take my child away from me?'

Her voice trembled, broke. 'Why would you blackmail me into marriage?'

Surprise and perhaps even regret flashed across Rafe's face, and then his expression hardened. 'I simply want what is best for our child,' he told her flatly. 'Isn't that what you want?'

'I want…' Freya stopped, for she knew what she wanted wasn't possible. Had never been possible since she'd last given in to temptation, wrecked three lives and destroyed another. *Love.* Happiness. A family. None of those were possible for her—except, amazingly, the last. Yet not in a way she had ever envisaged or would have chosen. Still, she acknowledged bleakly, it was the only option. Her only chance at some kind of happiness.

She would not risk losing her child in a custody battle; she would not have her past raked up in the courts—perhaps even the tabloids, considering Rafe's fame and fortune. If that happened she could only imagine how the courts would decide…and it wouldn't be in her favour.

No, she knew what she would do—what she had to do, even if it felt like tearing her heart in two. 'Fine,' she said, her voice barely audible. 'I'll do it.'

She would marry Rafe. Rafe gave her a grim smile of satisfaction, but she knew the bleakness in his eyes mirrored her own. This was not a situation either of them had envisaged—or wanted.

CHAPTER NINE

'GOOD morning.' The doctor, a middle-aged woman with a neat bun of black hair, bustled into the examining room in the modern office block in Seville.

Freya murmured a greeting back, conscious of the vulnerability of her situation, of Rafe's looming presence in the corner of the room, and of the memories.

Oh, the memories.

They crouched in the corners, crowded *her*. Overwhelmed her. The antiseptic smell, the churning fear, the utter hopelessness. She'd tried to prepare herself for this moment, but the sights and sounds brought it all rushing back so she could barely keep herself from losing her breakfast.

The doctor glanced at her in concern. 'Are you all right, *señora*?'

Freya did not bother to correct her. *Señorita*. Still single. 'I'm just a little dizzy, that's all,' she whispered. She knew she must look deathly pale.

Rafe's brows snapped together in concern, and to her surprise he brought out a packet of semi-mashed crackers from his pocket. 'Perhaps you should eat something,' he said gruffly, then added with a note of apology, 'That's all I have.'

Freya murmured her thanks, holding the crackers in one slick fist. She realised he must have brought them for her, and even in the midst of her emotional agony the thought comforted her.

'So.' The doctor reached for a clipboard and uncapped her pen. 'We should start with your history. Is this your first pregnancy?'

Freya stared at her sickly as the question reverberated through the little room. Her fist clenched, crushing the crackers to crumbs. Why had she not thought of this? Of *course* the doctor would want her history. Of *course* she needed to know everything.

Of course Rafe would find out.

Had she actually thought she could keep her secrets? Only yesterday she had told him that her secrets had nothing to do with him, yet here they were, filling the room with their malevolent memories, taking all the air. She struggled for a breath, knowing she would never escape her past, or the consequences of her own rash actions.

'*Señora?*' the doctor prompted gently. 'Would you like a drink of water?'

She flicked a glance at Rafe, who was glowering as he stood by the door, sensing something was wrong. Freya could only imagine how angry he would be. He would feel deceived…again. The injustice of it brought tears stinging to her eyes—because she had not anticipated this, had not wanted it to happen like this. Yet still she accepted the futile inevitability of the moment, of the truth.

The doctor cleared her throat. 'Would you like to conduct this examination alone?'

Freya shook her head, knowing there was no point. She couldn't keep the truth from Rafe the way Rosalia had. She would have to reveal her secrets after all. 'No. It's fine.' She cleared her throat. 'This isn't my first pregnancy.'

She felt Rafe's shock as if she were electrically wired to him—felt its painful current pulse through her own body even though he hid his reaction. He didn't even move. In fact he went very, very still.

The doctor smiled encouragingly, her gaze firmly focused on Freya. 'When were your previous pregnancies?'

'There was only one,' Freya said. She felt numb now, and she faced the doctor directly, refusing to look at Rafe. 'Ten years ago.'

'And it went full-term?'

'No.' She swallowed, took a breath. 'I had a termination at eleven weeks.'

Rafe must have made some sound, although Freya wasn't sure what it was. She didn't look at him as he murmured his excuses and quietly left the room. She stared down at her lap.

'I'm sorry,' the doctor murmured. 'Was your husband not aware of this?'

Freya shook her head. She didn't have the strength to say that Rafe wasn't her husband even though he soon would be. Unless, of course, he'd changed his mind. Bleakly she wondered if she'd just lost her chance at the slender thread of happiness her pregnancy had offered.

Rafe strode through the office corridor and burst through the waiting room doors. The sun was shining, the sky a hard, brilliant blue. People strolled by, enjoying the spring afternoon. Rafe turned down the street, walking quickly, his head down, emotions rolling through him. Shock. Anger. Disappointment. *Hurt.*

Freya had lied. Lied just like his mother, telling him she didn't know why his father hated him so much. Like Rosalia, insisting she didn't know why she couldn't get pregnant. He'd known Freya had been hiding something—but this?

Why? Her lie was as senseless as Rosalia's. Why tell him she was infertile when she'd fallen pregnant before? Why had his wife told him she would fall pregnant when she'd been on birth control the entire time? Why was he deceived again and again? What was *wrong* with him?

A coldly logical part of his mind told him that Freya had not lied the way Rosalia had. In fact she'd told the truth as soon as she'd been asked; there really hadn't been a moment to volunteer such painful, personal information before. He did not know when she'd been told she was infertile; most likely it had been after the last pregnancy. He *knew* that. And yet he could not keep himself from feeling tricked. Betrayed.

Hurt.

He walked all the way to the Alcazar Gardens, behind Seville's ancient Moorish palace. He strode past pavilions and fountains, oblivious to their beauty and history. Finally he sat on a stone bench and stared blindly in front of him. He realised, distantly, that he must have been gone for half an hour or more. Freya might be waiting for him, wondering where he was. Stranded. Still he didn't move.

His body and mind ached with this new knowledge. He understood, at least in part, that this wasn't even about Freya—not completely. Her admission had brought all his own painful memories to the fore. His mother's deceit. His father's rejection. His wife's betrayal.

'You should have taken care of it rather than live with the shame.'

His father's hissed voice, in an argument with his mother, burst into his brain. He hadn't even realised he'd remembered it. Only later had he understood what his father meant—that he'd been talking about Rafe. The unwanted child.

And Rosalia's lies—over and over again. *'I don't know why I can't fall pregnant. I don't want to see a doctor.'* And finally, before she'd left, *'I never wanted your baby, Rafe.'* And she'd been pregnant at the time. What burning need for vengeance had driven her to deceive him so terribly, for so long?

And what of Freya? He thought of her pale, stricken face in the doctor's office. Ten years ago she'd been no more than a teenager. What had happened? Had she loved the father? Jealousy twined around his heart, his lungs, stealing his breath. He had never felt it so fiercely before, for a man who was no longer in Freya's life. The realisation was shaming. Yet that man had been the father of her unborn child.

He stood up suddenly, needing to move. The thought of Freya loving someone, losing him, losing her baby, filled him with an unreasonable fury. It had happened ten years ago, and yet the knowledge was fresh. It hurt him, and he did not like to think why. Her past actions surely shouldn't affect his feelings now. Their marriage was to be a business arrangement, not a love-match. It had to be.

Freya sat hunched on one of the chairs in the waiting room, looking at no one, feeling nothing. Or trying to. When she'd come out of the exam room Rafe had been nowhere in sight. She'd realised she wasn't even surprised. She wondered if he'd left her here for good, cut her out completely. Her unexpected news would not have been received well by a traditional, family-centred man like Rafe. And of course he would have expected her to tell him yesterday, when he'd demanded to know her secrets. Well, now he knew. The question was, what was he going to do about it?

She'd wait an hour, she decided. And then she'd take a taxi back to his villa. After that, she couldn't think what she'd do. What Rafe would demand.

Things really didn't change, she thought grimly. Ten years ago she'd been hunched in an office like this one, the knowledge of her pregnancy like a stone inside her, with nowhere to go, no hope at all.

'We don't want to see you again. Don't attempt to contact us.'

She forced it back—all of it. At least she was older, wiser, and she was keeping this baby…if Rafe let her.

'Are you all right?'

Freya looked up to see Rafe standing there, his hands shoved in his pockets, his face pale and grim. She nodded, then stood. She felt as fragile as glass, as insubstantial as a breath of wind, but she would not let him know. He held out his hand, and after a second's hesitation Freya took it. The contact surprised her; she hadn't expected Rafe to reach out to her at all. She hadn't expected to take his hand. Yet the feel of it encasing hers was like being thrown an anchor in a drowning sea. She clung to it.

Silently they walked to the car. Rafe opened the passenger door and Freya slid in with murmured thanks; she sounded normal. She sounded fine. It amazed her, because she felt as if she were falling apart, as if she were nothing but fragments.

Rafe got in the driver's side. He sat there for a moment, silent, unmoving, his hands resting lightly on the steering wheel. 'The pregnancy?' he finally asked. 'Is everything…?'

'Fine.' Freya turned her face to the window. 'Everything's fine.'

They didn't speak all the way back to the villa.

Freya went directly to Max as soon as they returned; Damita had been looking after him, but he threw himself happily into her arms and asked if they could go swimming.

'Of course we can,' Freya said, hugging him back, grateful for his easy joy and childish warmth. She needed that respite now.

'And Rafe? Will he come too?'

She swallowed, her throat suddenly tight. 'I think Rafe might be busy this afternoon, *cariño*.'

Max's face fell for a moment, but then he shrugged and

tugged on her hand. 'Oh, well. He'll come later. He always does.'

They spent most of the afternoon outside, and just as always Rafe appeared towards the end of the day. He wore swimming trunks, and Freya's breath caught in her throat at the sight of his bare chest, at the broad golden expanse of his back tapering down to trim hips. He didn't even look her way as he swam towards Max and began to play with him, tossing him up in the air much to the little boy's delight.

Freya sat on the edge of the pool, her arms crossed in front of her breasts, trying to look relaxed and unconcerned, as if Rafe's nearness didn't cause an ache of longing to go through her. As if she wasn't waiting for her world to implode when Rafe turned to her and said there would be no marriage. No family. *He* would retain custody of their child.

She feared the worst; of course she did. The worst had happened before.

She closed her eyes, swamped with sorrow. She'd kept herself apart for so long, buried herself in mathematics and the cool logic of numbers as a way to distance herself from any kind of relationship at all…until she'd seen that advert for a nanny for Max and hadn't been able to resist the thought of finally caring for someone. For a child. Yet look where it had got her. Once again she'd succumbed to temptation. Once again she'd fallen into that old trap.

She would never find happiness or love—not with guilt eating away her insides, sorrow heavy inside her like a stone.

'Freya?'

Her eyes flew open. Rafe stood in front of her, Max clinging to him like a monkey.

'You look pale. Perhaps you should get out of the pool. I'll get Max ready for dinner.'

He kept his voice neutral, but his eyes were dark…with

coldness or with concern Freya couldn't tell. She did not want to know.

She nodded, too weakened by her own misery even to attempt to pretend to pull herself together.

Back in her room she fell into a restless doze, waking to find the hour late. Dinner had passed and Max was most likely asleep. Freya slipped out to the garden, wandering the stone paths that wound through orange and olive trees, clumps of broom and prickly pear, softened by the climbing honeysuckle, its sweet scent drifting on the night breeze.

She ended up in an enclosed garden, with a magnificent mosaic-tiled fountain its centerpiece. The burbling sound of the water was soothing in the silence of the night.

Freya didn't know how long she sat there, her knees curled up to her chest, her chin resting on top. She let the sounds of wind and water fill her mind, empty it out. Then she heard another sound—the crunch of feet on gravel—and turned to see Rafe standing in the entrance to the garden, no more than a shadow in the darkness.

Neither of them spoke. The silence felt heavy, weighted with expectation. Freya turned her head away from Rafe.

'I wondered where you'd gone,' he finally said.

'I just wanted some air.' Her whole body tensed for the hammer blow.

I've decided not to marry you after all. I'll take custody of our child. You'll never see Max again.

Rafe didn't speak, and Freya was wondering if he'd actually turned around and left when she felt him sit next to her on the bench. Awareness and shock rippled through her; he was close enough that his hip nudged her own. She kept her face averted, afraid of what he might see there.

The moon emerged from behind a cloud, and in its silver wash Freya knew her face was illuminated. Her breath came out in a rush of surprise when Rafe's thumb touched her cheek.

'You're crying.'

'Am I?' Humiliation flowed through her. She hadn't even known she had tears streaking down her face. She dashed at her cheeks with her palms, still trying to keep her face turned away from Rafe.

'Freya…' He spoke softly, his tone quiet, serious, perhaps even sad.

Freya tensed. She didn't think she wanted to hear what he had to say.

In the end he didn't say anything at all. His hands stole around her shoulders and he pulled her into his arms. It took Freya a stunned moment to realise what was happening: he was hugging her.

Her body resisted, tensing, trying to pull away, but her mind and heart needed this contact, this comfort, too much. She could hardly believe it was coming from Rafe.

After a second when neither of them moved Freya relaxed into Rafe's embrace, her head against his shoulder, her cheek on his chest, and as Rafe stroked her hair the tears she'd been trying to suppress for ten endless years finally came in a hot, healing rush.

CHAPTER TEN

ONCE the tears came, it felt impossible to stop them. Freya's shoulders shook and her breath came in hiccuppy gasps as Rafe stroked her hair. Distantly she realised he was murmuring endearments: *cariña, querida, mi corazón.* My heart.

She'd expected condemnation, not comfort. Rejection instead of acceptance. And yet he still didn't know the whole truth.

And when he did...

She pulled away, wiping her cheeks, trying desperately to pass off this moment as a temporary weakness rather than a life-shattering event. 'I'm sorry,' she finally managed in a wobbly voice. 'You probably weren't expecting that.'

'I've come to realise I don't know *what* to expect,' Rafe said.

He didn't sound condemning, yet she still heard a thread of steel in his voice. He wanted answers.

'Freya?' he said, and waited.

She looked away, knowing she had to tell him. She wanted to tell him. She was so tired of secrets; she'd kept them for so long, and they were such a heavy burden to bear alone. Yet her throat was so tight and aching she could barely force the words out.

'I went to Spain for my gap year,' she began hesitantly. She kept her face averted. 'I was so excited. I'd done an

A-Level in Spanish and I really wanted to become fluent. And see Spain, of course. I thought it was going to be such a grand adventure.'

She paused, biting her lip, and Rafe waited. 'I lived with a young couple—Anita and Timeo.' It hurt to say their names even now. 'They were so glamorous and fun. It was a whole new world for me. My parents had me later in life, and they've always been very formal. Traditional. Wonderful, but not fun like that.' She stopped, not wanting to go on.

'And?' Rafe prompted quietly, when the silence had stretched to several minutes.

'I was stupid,' Freya said in a low voice. 'Really, really stupid—and selfish and naive, too, I suppose.' She shook her head. 'Anita was a doctor, and she worked all sorts of late hours. Timeo was a freelance photographer, and he was often home during the day. He was—he seemed very kind.' She felt Rafe tense, knew he'd started to suspect where this was going. 'I let my head be turned,' Freya said, her voice thick with bitterness and self-loathing. 'And—and more than that. The worst.'

Rafe remained very still, yet Freya felt as if he'd moved away from her. Withdrawn now that he was learning the truth. And why shouldn't he?

'I was old enough to know better. I know I was. But I listened to all the things Timeo said—that I was beautiful, that he wasn't happy with Anita…' She shook her head, felt the hot sting of tears under her lids once again. 'I bought into it all.' She stopped, not wanting to go on.

'And?' Rafe asked, his voice very low.

'And we had an affair,' Freya said dully. 'For several months.' Even now, ten years later, it sounded so sordid. She would never be free. 'Until I fell pregnant.'

'What happened then?' Rafe asked.

His voice was toneless, so Freya couldn't tell what he thought. Felt. She could only imagine.

'Anita found out. She recognised the signs before I did, actually. Just like you did. She guessed right away. I've sometimes wondered if—if I wasn't the first. In any case, she wanted me out of there. She drove me to a doctor—at least I think she was a doctor.'

Freya shivered, the memories making her cold to her soul. She'd never told anyone so much—not even her parents. She knew they wouldn't have been able to handle the truth; what they'd known had been bad enough. And even though she knew she was damning herself with every word, it felt good to tell someone. Tell Rafe. Like lancing a boil.

'She was awful,' she whispered. 'She performed the termination. I was in such a daze I couldn't even *think*…' She swallowed, then said in a voice so low it was barely audible, 'Sometimes I wish I could go back and have that moment over again. I'd choose differently. Except it didn't even feel like a choice. Not for me.'

Rafe was silent for another long moment. Freya wished she knew what he was thinking, but she was afraid to look him in the face.

'Terminations were illegal in Spain then,' he finally said, without any expression at all.

'I know. Anita had a connection somehow—it wasn't in a normal office, and it was…awful.' She shook her head, not wanting to say any more. She still had nightmares about that room, the blood. 'I didn't want to tell my parents any of it. I knew it would be horrible for them, and I was so ashamed.' She drew in a ragged breath. 'But in the end I developed a severe infection, and they had to come to Spain to fetch me home.'

She didn't go into details—didn't want to tell Rafe the want truth. How Anita had thrown her out and she'd had nowhere to stay. She'd been picked up by the police for sleeping on a park bench, feverish and delirious, full of shame and guilt. It had been the lowest point of her life.

'That's why I didn't think I could have children—I had scarring from the procedure. They told me I was infertile.'

Rafe was silent for a long moment. Freya's nails bit into her palms as she waited for his verdict. *This changes everything. I can't marry you now. You'll leave immediately.*

'So,' he said slowly, and Freya closed her eyes, waiting, *aching*, 'this baby really is a miracle.'

Her breath came out in a ragged gasp of shock and gratitude and tears slipped down her cheeks. It was just about the last thing she'd expected him to say. 'Yes…' she managed. 'I hope so. I hope this baby can banish what happened before. I know I can never actually forget, but to not always remember—' She stopped, wiping her cheeks. 'No one tells you how awful it is. How you keep *thinking*—'

Rafe pulled her to him, and Freya did not resist. She needed his touch, craved it. Yet she wanted more, longed for absolution, or perhaps just obliteration. Some deep need inside her compelled her to lift her face up to his, and when she felt his hesitation she closed the distance between their mouths and kissed him with all the desperation she felt.

She felt Rafe tense in surprise, and she pulled him closer to her, threading her fingers through his hair. After another taut second Rafe responded, his mouth opening to hers, and desire and relief flooded through Freya in equal amounts. She *needed* this. Needed this comfort, this closeness.

'No.'

Rafe pulled away, his breathing ragged, and desolation swamped her soul once again. He was disgusted by her, no matter what he'd said.

'Not like this. Not like—' He stopped, but Freya knew what he was thinking. Remembering. *Not like last time.* And she knew, despite the desire coursing through her, that he was right. Sex was only a temporary release. Regret came after. Yet she didn't want him to go.

'Rafe—'

'You need to rest,' Rafe said. 'There will be time to—to talk through things later.'

Freya didn't know if they were, but his words felt like a rejection. She didn't need to rest; she needed Rafe.

'All right,' she whispered, because she didn't want to admit how much she needed him. Wanted him. She felt his emotional withdrawal like a physical thing–a coldness in the air, in herself.

He rose from the bench and she followed him out of the darkness of the garden into the villa. He paused on the threshold of his study, his expression shadowed, unfathomable. 'Goodnight,' he said.

The word sounded final somehow, and Freya did not have the strength to respond. She simply nodded, her heart aching, and turned to the stairs. Behind her she heard the door to Rafe's study click shut, and it felt as if something far greater was being closed. The door to his heart, to hope. She had not been imagining the coolness in his gaze, the way he'd distanced himself.

In her bedroom she undressed and slid between the cool sheets. She felt emotionally exhausted from her confession, and yet her mind and heart seethed with anxious uncertainty about the future.

For a moment—a wonderful moment—she'd felt forgiven. *This baby really is a miracle.*

Rafe had offered her comfort in that moment of desolation, but that was all it had been. A moment. Moments, Freya thought bleakly, seemed like all she would ever have.

Lying there in the darkness of her bedroom, she knew her feelings for Rafe were deeper and stronger than she could ever let him know. She loved him—loved his gentleness with Max, loved the kindness and sensitivity she knew was inside him even though the anger and suspicion he still harboured from his unhappy marriage hid them at times. Lying there, tears streaking silently down her cheeks, Freya knew what she wanted. What she'd never felt she deserved.

She wanted love. Marriage, children–everything. And she wanted it with Rafe. The only problem—the huge, agonising dilemma—was that she was desperately afraid he didn't want the same. And after he'd thought about all she'd confessed, Freya wondered if tomorrow Rafe would send her away for ever.

Alone in his study, Rafe stared sightlessly in front of him as all Freya had said—*confessed*—echoed through his mind. And his heart. He was shaken by what she'd endured, what it had made him feel. Anger. Sorrow. Regret.

Guilt.

The last emotion surprised him, because he realised in all the years of his marriage, and all the years after, he'd never felt guilty. Confused, enraged, even sad and despairing. But guilty? No. He'd never thought he had anything to be guilty about. Rosalia was the one who had lied to him. She'd tricked him for five years, and then wounded him in the worst way possible.

'I never wanted your baby, Rafe. I never told you because I knew you'd divorce me.' The words had been snarled, punctuated by sobs, a testament to Rosalia's anger and grief, and yet Rafe had never let himself think what her admission said about *him*.

Now, in light of Freya's own honesty, he knew he needed to be honest with himself. About himself. What kind of man had Rosalia thought he was? What kind of man had he *been*? For the very fact that Rosalia had been so afraid of his rejection made Rafe realise how cold-hearted and single-minded he must have seemed to her all the years of their marriage. He'd been obsessed with having a child, with creating a family to replace the one he'd had… A mother who couldn't look at him because he reminded her of her own shame—a father who hated him and never told him why. And he'd thought marriage and a family of his own would wipe away those sins. Those sorrows.

He'd never been more wrong.

His marriage to Rosalia had been a mistake, and one that had cost both of them their happiness. He'd never loved her—not the way he should have. She'd simply, Rafe acknowledged bleakly, been the expedient means to an end. And she must have known. He'd told her from the beginning that he wanted children as soon as possible. Had she agreed? Had she lied then? Rafe didn't know anymore.

She had only been twenty years old, beautiful, young, orphaned. Her mother had died—in childbirth. That must have contributed to her reluctance to have children, yet Rafe had never given it a thought. He hadn't given Rosalia much of a thought, he acknowledged grimly. He'd been consumed with his work, with establishing himself, with proving to his father and the world that he was worthy.

And the result had been success—and tragedy.

Now, instead of feeling angry at her deception, he felt the lacerating pain of guilt for his own part in the tragedy of their marriage. And Freya had been living with guilt for so long—guilt for poor choices, terrible mistakes. She needed, Rafe knew, to let go of her guilt. He needed to accept his.

And they both needed to move on. Yet how? How could he contemplate another marriage when his first had been such a failure? How could he make the same mistake twice? Entering into a loveless union for the sake of a child, or the hope of a child?

Rafe drove his fingers through his hair and let out a weary sigh. He thought of Freya's choked words, her desperate kiss, the softness of her hair and her skin as she twined her arms around him. He'd wanted to kiss her back. He'd wanted to make love to her properly, not something rushed and regrettable like before. He'd wanted to love her.

Love her.

The word stilled him. Could he love her? *Did* he? After the failure of his marriage, Rafe wasn't even sure he knew how to love. Yet he knew he could no longer imagine a life without Freya—without her tender smile, her cool gaze, the sudden warmth of her embrace. He needed her in his life, in Max's life. Their unborn child's life.

Their family's life.

Rafe dropped his hands and took a deep breath, letting it out slowly. Freya had given him something precious and dangerous tonight: her honesty. Her vulnerability. She'd given him the secrets he'd demanded, and now Rafe knew what he had to do. He needed to give her his.

Yet even as this knowledge thudded through him he remained motionless, in conflict, *afraid* as he stared out at the unrelenting darkness of the night.

CHAPTER ELEVEN

FREYA woke to sunlight streaming through the windows and a still-aching heart. The memories of last night—and its possible repercussions—tumbled through her mind and made her close her eyes once more. She did not want to get up. She did not want to face Rafe and his possible rejection. *Likely* rejection, considering how he'd withdrawn from her last night. She still recalled her own desperate kiss—did she *never* learn?—and Rafe's refusal. The shuttered look in his eyes, the way he'd closed the door.

She could hear Max starting to stir in the adjoining nursery, and Freya rose from the bed and dressed, her limbs leaden and as heavy as her heart. She was just about to open the door to the nursery when a deep, masculine voice startled her, stopping her in her tracks.

'Good morning, Max.'

'Rafe!' Max exclaimed, clearly happy to see him. 'Where's Freya?'

'Still sleeping, I imagine. But you're going to stay with Damita today. She wants your help making *mallorquinas*. How would you like that?'

Freya barely heard Max's excited reply; the dark chocolate cookies were his new favourite. All she could register was the fact that Rafe was already cutting her out of Max's life, no doubt making arrangements for her departure. She closed her eyes, nausea that had nothing to do with her pregnancy rising in her throat. So quick. So terrible. Yet what else could she expect from El Tiburón?

She waited a moment to get her emotions and expression under control, and then opened the door, even managing a cool smile directed at Rafe. 'Good morning.'

'Freya!' Max tackled her around the knees. 'I'm making *mallor—mallor—*'

'*Mallorquinas,*' Rafe prompted with a chuckle.

He raised his head to look at Freya and she felt her face drain of colour at the grim determination in his hooded gaze. 'We need to talk.'

She nodded numbly, not trusting herself to speak. They all went down to breakfast, yet Freya was barely conscious of Max's happy chatter, and she ate next to nothing. All she could feel were the minutes and hours ticking away until Rafe told her to leave.

For surely that was what he intended to say. There could surely be no mistaking his moody silence, the occasional frowning glances he directed her way, or the unalterable and ominous fact that he'd arranged for Max to spend the day with Damita. He wanted her gone.

Bile rose in her throat and she pushed away from the table. 'Excuse me.' She barely made it to the bathroom before she retched helplessly, tears starting in her eyes. She blinked them back fiercely, longing for that distant composure she'd worn for so many years, now utterly beyond her. Too much had happened—too much had been lost—for her to attempt to hide behind a cool smile.

'Freya?' She heard Rafe from behind the bathroom door and quickly rinsed her mouth out, washed her face and hands.

'Sorry,' she murmured, pushing past him, but Rafe touched

her shoulder, stilling her. The simple contact reverberated through her body with longing and loss.

'I thought we'd go out,' he said, and Freya nodded jerkily. 'Fine.'

'Freya—' He stopped, and she just shook her head.

'I'll be ready in a few minutes.'

Fifteen minutes later they were driving along twisting roads towards Granada, the sun blazing down and touching the rocky hills in gold. Freya said nothing, her face turned towards the window, and Rafe seemed disinclined to talk as well.

He parked by the Plaza Nueva in Granada, turning to Freya for the first time since they'd got in the car. 'We can walk to the Alhambra if you don't mind a bit of an ascent.'

Freya shrugged. She hardly cared where they went; she wondered why Rafe was making such an effort. Perhaps he wanted to tell her in a public place, to make sure she wouldn't make a scene? Didn't he know her well enough by now? She never made scenes, even if her heart was breaking the way it had ten years ago. The way it was now.

They walked up a broad, ancient avenue, shaded from the sun by towering elms, with the gardens of the Alhambra spread out on terraced lawns before them. It was all stunningly beautiful, yet for Freya it might as well have been a prison cell. She felt as if the cell doors were slowly but surely closing with every step she took. It was simply a matter of how Rafe chose to imprison her: a loveless marriage, separation from Max or, worst of all, a fight for custody of her own child. Tears started again in her eyes and she turned her face away from Rafe.

'These gardens are very peaceful,' he murmured as they left the avenue to stroll along the terraces.

Freya let out a choked laugh. Nothing felt peaceful about this moment; he was about to take her life apart.

'Freya?' he said, and she turned to him.

'Let's not postpone this, Rafe,' she said in a low voice. 'Just say what you came to say.' She kept her head down, afraid he'd see the tears glittering in her eyes.

Rafe didn't speak for a long moment, and when Freya risked a glance upwards she saw him gazing at her in sorrowful bemusement. 'I think,' he said, 'what I came to say is not what you are expecting me to say.'

'What does it matter?' she asked rawly. 'It can't be good.'

'No?' Rafe still sounded bemused, and although she wasn't looking at him she felt his fingers, cool and strong, touch her chin and turn her face up to his. 'I suppose I should let you be the judge of whether it is good,' he said. 'I came here to tell you I love you.'

Freya could only stare. His words reverberated through her, but they didn't make sense. They couldn't. Surely he didn't mean…? Was this a joke? A trap? 'No…'

He raised his eyebrows. 'Not the reaction I was hoping for, actually.'

'But… Last night you left me so suddenly, and you looked so serious, and then you made Max go with Damita—'

'So we could be alone today,' Rafe said. 'And last night I left because I had a lot to think about. A lot of things to accept.'

'About me?'

'About *me*,' Rafe corrected gently. 'And *my* actions.' He touched her face, his palm cupping her cheek, his thumb brushing away her tears. 'Freya, you've been consumed by guilt for so long, and surely ten years' penance is enough. Too much. You need to forgive yourself.'

Forgive. It was all so unexpected, so wonderful. She felt the first stirrings of absolution. 'But—'

'And I needed to accept guilt for my part in the failure of my marriage.' Rafe let out a long, ragged breath. 'I've been

consumed by anger for so long, full of self-righteous fury.'
He shook his head. 'When you told me your story, and I
saw how guilty you felt still, it made me think about how I
didn't feel guilty when perhaps I should. I surely had a part
in the sorry state of affairs. Rosalia was so young when she
married me, and I didn't love her the way I should have. The
way I love *you*.'

Freya swiped at her cheeks, her disbelief turning to an
incredulous dawning joy. 'I thought you were going to tell
me to go,' she whispered.

He looked startled, his brows snapping together, before
regret shadowed his eyes and he shook his head. 'I'm sorry.
I didn't realize…' He let out a slow breath. 'I never should
have threatened you with some kind of custody battle—especially now that I know what you endured before. I was
speaking out of anger and fear. I'm sorry.'

Freya felt as if her mind were spinning, as if her heart
had been given wings, and yet hope still felt like a dangerous thing. 'I thought—after I told you—' She looked down,
unable to continue, and stiffened in surprise when she felt
Rafe's arms close around her.

'Oh, Freya,' he murmured. 'What you endured was terrible, but it showed me the person you are—the person you've
become. Brave and strong and gentle and true. Do you think
I am going to hold what happened ten years ago against you
now? Against who you are now?'

She shook her head, her cheek pressed against his chest.

Rafe let out a little sigh. 'I suppose you have good reason
to think I would,' he admitted quietly. 'I held Rosalia's deception against her for so long, yet last night I started to
think about how I contributed to it. I wanted a child so much,
too much perhaps, and for a lot of convoluted reasons.' He
shook his head sorrowfully. 'In part because my own childhood was so unhappy, and because I felt so rejected by my

own father. I wanted to prove to him that I could have a family of my own, that I could have everything he'd denied me. And I think I thought having a child would somehow help to heal my own past. But it didn't, of course, because I held on to my anger.'

'How—how did your father reject you?' Freya whispered. 'Why?'

'My mother never told me the truth about my father. She was pregnant by another man when she married him—that was why she married him. She didn't tell him, but he found out eventually. I don't know how.' His arms tightened around her. 'I don't suppose it really matters. What mattered to me, as a child, was that he never loved me. Never even liked me. He treated me like a stranger inhabiting his house. I never understood it. And my mother never told me why. I can understand why she didn't, yet still—she seemed ashamed of me. I think she was probably ashamed of herself. But as a child—'

His voice caught, and Freya pulled him closer.

'My father finally told me,' he said quietly. 'When I was eighteen. He'd done his duty by me, or so he seemed to think, and he cut me off without a penny and of course with no inheritance. I made my own way, and I was glad—determined—to do so. But I still wanted my own family—maybe just to prove something to my father, or to myself. I don't know.' He let out another weary sigh, resting his chin on top of her head. 'But obviously I married for the wrong reasons, and doomed my marriage to failure with my single-minded purpose.'

'You can't blame yourself completely.'

'And neither can you. We can both accept our guilt and then move on. Forgiveness doesn't come without that.' He tilted her chin so she was gazing up at him again, and she saw his face soften with warmth, with acceptance, with love.

'I love you and I want us to have a real marriage. A real family. Do you want that?'

Freya's throat was tight with tears, so she could only nod. He brushed her damp cheek with his thumb.

'You're crying.'

'I seem to be doing that a lot lately,' she admitted with a shaky laugh. 'And after not crying for so long. But these are good tears.'

'When I first met you,' Rafe said, 'I thought you were so controlled, so cold. You didn't seem to have any emotion at all. And there I was, boiling with rage and fear and desire.'

Freya laughed softly. 'Desire?'

'Yes—for you. From just about the first moment I saw you in that boring black skirt. You made it look very sexy.'

'You're right, though,' Freya confessed quietly. 'I'd almost fooled myself into thinking I didn't feel anything at all. I didn't want to feel because I knew it would hurt. And yet from just about the first moment I met you you *made* me feel. So much. And that was very scary.'

'It still is a little bit, isn't it?' Rafe said soberly. 'I was scared to tell you I loved you—that's why I looked so grim this morning.'

'And now?' Freya asked with a tremulous smile.

'Now,' he said, 'I'm a very happy man.'

Rafe tipped her chin up so their eyes met, and then their lips did, in a soft, sweet kiss that made every part of her ache.

The kiss was a promise, a balm, and it told Freya that the past really was finished. Forgiven. And the future lay before them—bright, shining and new.

* * * * *

Harlequin *Presents*

Coming Next Month

from **Harlequin Presents® EXTRA.** Available September 13, 2011.

#165 HIS UNKNOWN HEIR
Chantelle Shaw
Aristocrats' Reluctant Brides

#166 WIFE IN THE SHADOWS
Sara Craven
Aristocrats' Reluctant Brides

#167 MAHARAJA'S MISTRESS
Susan Stephens
Young, Hot & Royal

#168 THE CROWN AFFAIR
Lucy King
Young, Hot & Royal

Coming Next Month

from **Harlequin Presents®.** Available September 27, 2011.

#3017 THE COSTARELLA CONQUEST
Emma Darcy

#3018 THE FEARLESS MAVERICK
Robyn Grady
The Notorious Wolfes

#3019 THE KANELLIS SCANDAL
Michelle Reid

#3020 HEART OF THE DESERT
Carol Marinelli

#3021 DOUKAKIS'S APPRENTICE
Sarah Morgan
21st Century Bosses

#3022 AN INCONVENIENT OBSESSION
Natasha Tate

Visit www.HarlequinInsideRomance.com
for more information on upcoming titles!

HPCNM0911